MW00513799

CAVE OF ICE

Penelope Mortimer's uncanny faculty for evoking intense drama from the conflicts that lie beneath the surface of middle-class domesticity is strikingly displayed in *Cave of Ice.*

Mrs. Mortimer turns her relentless gaze on a suburban enclave fifty miles from London, where prosperous professional men, five days out of the week, leave wives and offspring to their own devices. Several marriages are examined with dispassionate wit. The center of the stage, however, is occupied by the Whiting family, whose five members arouse our pity, our terror—and our laughter.

Rex, the bullying husband; Ruth, whose eighteen years of matrimony have been one long attempt to escape reality; Angela, confronted with an appalling dilemma; her two schoolboy brothers, blithely unaware that history, for their elders, has frighteningly begun to repeat itself: we follow them all with fascinated attention. And the central story, in whose course at least one human being starts coming to terms with life, is augmented by a series of ironic variations, played out by men and women drawn with Penelope Mortimer's customary acuity and humor.

An unflinchingly honest book, *Cave of Ice* is the most dramatic and moving novel yet written by a notably gifted member of the new generation of writers.

Also by Penelope Mortimer

A VILLA IN SUMMER

THE BRIGHT PRISON

CAVE OF ICE

Penelope Mortimer

"It was a miracle of rare device,
A sunny pleasure-dome with caves of ice . . ."

Harcourt, Brace and Company
New York

CAVE OF ICE

R UTH WHITING stepped out of the high train directly it stopped. She had collected her parcels together, the ornamental carrier bags and discreet cardboard boxes from Knightsbridge, as the train passed the cemetery. She had stood by the door, her ticket tucked in her glove, the parcels arranged on the seat, loops and handles uppermost, so that she would lose no time. Ramsbridge was a terminus station. Even if she had found herself locked in the carriage there would have been no danger. If she had been in a hurry she might have appeared anxious, bundled her packages together for a clumsy jump on to the platform. She was not in a hurry. She was simply in the dusty, lonely carriage, the transitory scene of slag heaps, black brick, advertisements for Mazawattee Tea and Virol, trying to establish order.

This particular journey, after sending the children back to school, was always unbearable. On the way up to London the carriage would be full, the two boys filling it with their legs and feet, the holiday-scarred knees and new, heavy shoes, their bodies, above these long, bony, curiously-clothed extremities, small and slumped, wearing blazers either too small or too big for them; their hands resting aimlessly in their laps without the energy to unscrew a toffee paper or turn the pages of the reputable comics she had bought for them. The conversation was nervous, desultory and, to all three of them, a strain. Everything was directed to the moment of parting, the moment when the other train, larger, more powerful, more cruel than this one, would stream out into the misty sunlight beyond Waterloo, the two insect arms waving until they were pulled briskly inside.

Ruth would hold up her hand until the train was out of sight, not waving, but raised like a timid and awkward blessing. When she turned back, it was to a world without discipline or purpose. This was why she did so much shopping. On the return journey the packages furnished the silent carriage, the empty car; they had to be unpacked and put away, made use of in the following days; they were her guarantee for the future.

She was first up the platform, the rap of her high heels followed by the tired shuffle of a few commuters, four or five prematurely old businessmen who had decided, for reasons of economy or health or cowardice, that it was reasonable to travel a hundred miles a day. She was through the barrier—her wrist held out with a charming, almost coquettish gesture for the ticket to be removed from her glove, murmuring that yes, they got off all right, yes, it would seem funny without them—before the ragged file of drooping trilby hats and ex-army raincoats had crept past the hissing engine. She had packed herself into the car and was away before they had trailed out of the station, their eyes narrowed against the mild and unfamiliar sun, their pallid faces anxiously peering for the wives who might, with any luck, have come to meet them.

It was not until she turned off the main road that Ruth

slid down a little in her seat, loosened her hands on the steering wheel, sighed. It was autumn. The long, painful, frustrating summer was over: the summer of wet socks, of plimsolls fossilised by salt and sand; the summer of Wellington boots and Monopoly, bicycles left out in the rain and the steady, pungent smell of bubble gum; the summer of inadequacy. It had begun with strawberries pried out like jewels from under the wet leaves and covering of straw; it had ended with bitter quarrels about who should shred the runner beans, hard and brown as old leather. And now it was over. The children, the summer, gone.

The road climbed steeply between beech trees fired to copper and crimson. The air was smoky, catching the chest with the bitter taste of charred wood.

What remains? What is left for tomorrow?

Angela. Angela is still there. Why don't you think about Angela?

Even Rex had gone, thankfully returning to work, to his London flat, after the month of anguish and boredom that was known as his holiday. It was mid-week, and he could never manage to see the children off. He made up for it by telephoning them the night before. She could tell, by the rolled-up eyes, the exaggerated smiles, the gestures of laboured winding-up and slumping, as though dead from shock, against the wall, that he was telling his joke about the Matron, warning them not to eat too much, reminding them that he had told her to give them ten shillings each, which they were not to lose. Sometimes, after this telephone call, the older boy, Julian, disappeared and spent a tormented half-hour slashing at cow-parsley, mooching among the hens. This, all of it, was over.

She shivered, wondering whether Angela would have

thought of lighting a fire. At last she made herself think of Angela, who had been alone all day, who was waiting for her to come home. She tried to feel glad Angela would be there. She tried to feel grateful. Intently, she concentrated on the picture of Angela lighting the fire, her long hair hanging forward as she knelt in front of the grate, her long hands delicately picking up the coal piece by piece and arranging it, as though making a mosaic, on the pyramid of sticks; her long, narrow body in the black jeans and sombre sweater folded up, almost inconsiderable, on the hearthrug. The picture became alive. The weight of loneliness lifted. She drove faster. There was still Angela to care for, lighting the fire only just in time.

After a little while she began to sing, quietly, slightly off-key. When the boys sang in the car, she stayed silent. When she was alone she would go through all the songs she had learnt at school, 'Drink to Me Only,' 'The Lass of Richmond Hill,' 'Men of Harlech.' Sometimes she sang hymns or, if it was a particularly long and lonely journey, the whole of the *Te Deum*. Sometimes she counted men with dogs, men with beards, piebald horses, running up astronomical scores against herself. This evening, singing to give herself courage, she could hardly hear the sound of her voice above the climbing note of the car.

At the top of the hill the country opened out, a flat plateau of gorse and bramble and bracken crossed by narrow, unfenced roads. Up here the air was heavy with frost. It was not yet dark, but she switched on the sidelights and slowed down as a motorcycle turned into the road twenty yards ahead, accelerated and roared savagely to meet her. She caught sight of a boy with an enormous scarf wound round his neck, a pillioned girl with hair streaming, duffle-coated arms clasped tightly round his waist. As they shot past her the girl opened her mouth, twisted perilously and waved. As Ruth turned, the red rear-light was disappearing into the distance, had plunged into the woods, was gone.

So Angela wasn't lighting the fire after all. The house would be empty.

She turned at the cross-roads and drove slowly down the bumpy lane. The lights of the Tanners' house pricked through the high yew hedge, there were two cars parked in the drive. The Tanners had visitors. Should she stop there, ring the bell, venture the dim, untidy room, the indifferent strangers?

'I just met my daughter—' she could hear her little laugh, rather too eager, too insistent that this was a joke—'rushing past on the back of someone's Vespa. No, I haven't the faintest idea who he was. Some young man from Oxford, I imagine.' The implication would be, you know what these teen-age girls are, one simply has no control over them. Someone would ask her, not caring, how old Angela was and she would say eighteen and someone else, probably a woman, would say no, it wasn't possible that she had a daughter of eighteen and Richard Tanner would say ah, it was a *News of the World* case at the time.

In all the years of her marriage, a long war in which attack, if not happening, was always imminent, she had learned an expert cunning. The way to avoid being hurt, to dodge unhappiness, was to run away. Feelings of guilt and cowardice presented no problems that couldn't be overcome by dreams, by games, by the gentle sound of her own voice advising and rebuking her as she went about the house. 'Poor old Mum,' she had heard Julian saying to Angela, 'she's going a bit barmy.' She was still young and her apparently commonplace life was deep with fantasy, full of hiding-places, a maze of secrecy and deceit and hope tunnelled below the unvarying days.

She wouldn't go to the Tanners. The momentary temptation to expose herself, to try and contact other people, was overcome. Briskly, she changed gear and drove on, a bright little smile on her mouth as though, at the other end of the long drive, she expected to be welcomed.

Chapter 2

THERE WAS A NOTE from Angela on the kitchen table.

> *Tony turned up and we've gone off to taste the delights of Ramsbridge—Hope you don't mind—Cold meat in fridge—Don't wait up—Love A.* TURN OVER.

Obediently, Ruth turned the paper over.

> *Daddy 'phoned—will you ring him before 7? Tony says thanks for the tea—Hope the kids got off all right—Love A.*

Breathless with haste and importance. Who Tony was, where he had come from and why, was meant to be none of Ruth's business. Yet the feeling that it was her business, that her approval was needed, cried out in the amount of love, the necessity of covering the whole page with large, emphatic writing. The cold meat and the hope that the children got off all right were efforts at contact as hopeless and wild as the waving hand, the soundless cry as she disappeared at sixty miles an hour over the horizon.

Oh well. I suppose she'll be all right. She'll be all right.

She put the note down on the table and slowly pulled

off her gloves. A door upstairs swung on creaking hinges; the tap dripped. She was not sure whether she had actually spoken or whether she had simply heard her own thoughts. She went to the kitchen cupboard, took out the gin and vermouth and poured herself a drink.

'She took to drinking alone. She began talking to herself. That evening while her daughter was out with a young man called Tony—'

She got up quickly and began undoing her parcels, tweed for a new dress, bath towels named His and Hers, stockings, two pairs of pyjamas, a box of soap. Lastly, with care, she unwrapped a child's musical box.

It was a present for Jane Tanner's baby. She had heard its tune, curiously sad and lingering, tinkling in the depths of the toy shop where she had gone to replace missing parts of Julian's meccano. A stern little girl in thick pebble glasses was turning the handle.

It was a pretty thing, shaped like a cradle, decorated with tinsel and silver paper and lace. The little girl, in spite of her daunting appearance, was turning the handle with care.

'What is it? The tune, I mean?'

The little girl had listened intently, turning the handle first slower, then faster. The tune remained melancholy and sweet, a lament without bitterness.

'I should *think* it's "Bye Baby Bunting." But mind you, I'm not sure.'

'Do you want it?'

'You can have it, if you like. I'm seven, actually. Rather old for that sort of thing.'

So she had bought it, thinking it was for Jane Tanner's baby. Now she held it up and cautiously turned the handle.

The tune, picked up in the middle of a bar, was an insect requiem, desolate, thin as air.

Bye Baby Bunting,
Daddy's gone a-hunting . . .

As the little girl had done, she turned the handle at different speeds, stopping suddenly and listening to the last note, alert and intent, trying to catch it out. Inside the paper-and-lace cradle the pea-sized celluloid head was serenely sleeping. It was gummed to the coverlet, and had no body. The whole ingenious contrivance weighed, on the palm of her hand, no more than a matchbox.

When the telephone rang she took the toy with her into the hall, holding it while she picked up the receiver.

The voice shot at her. 'Hullo? Hullo?'

She sat down, putting the musical box on the table, feeling the lace between finger and thumb. Of course, she told herself, it's not real lace, probably some sort of plastic. Although it obviously isn't plastic. It's cotton and might have been made in Japan.

'Hullo? Are you there, Ruth? Hullo?'

'Yes, Rex, I'm here.'

'Didn't Angela give you the message? I asked you to ring me.'

'I'm sorry. I only just got in and the message was on the kitchen table. I only just came through the door.'

'You've been a hell of a long time. I waited in the flat till seven. Didn't you catch the 4.30?'

'Yes, but it was late, and the car wouldn't start.'

'What's wrong with the car?'

'I expect it was cold or something.' She picked up the

musical box and turned it upside down. It was made in Germany.

'I've got a 5.30 appointment tomorrow and then the Craxtons will be driving me down. We'll have a late dinner. Is that all right?'

'You mean the Craxtons will be staying for the weekend.'

'Yes.' A slight pause and then, heavily, 'Any objection?'

'No.'

'It'll give you someone to talk to. That's what you want, isn't it?'

She said nothing. If the cradle could be held steady, it could be played with one hand.

'We might ask the Tanners in for a drink on Sunday morning.'

'Yes. Angela's gone out with a boy called Tony.'

'What boy?'

'I don't know. I mean, I only know he's called Tony and he's got a motor bike.'

'Well, didn't she tell you?'

'No, I wasn't here.'

'You mean to say she went careering off with some boy without telling you?'

'No. She told me. She left a note. I just said so.'

'Well, who is this boy? Do you mean to say you don't know who he is?'

She shut her eyes, pressing her knees tightly together. 'No, Rex. I don't know who he is. Have you been very busy?'

'Very.'

How many incisors and canines explored, she wondered; how many careful excavations into rotting bone, how much drilling on the nerve, how many bleeding cavities after

Craxton's neat injection of pentothal? She swallowed, opening her eyes and moving nervously forward on her chair.

'Well, that's good. I'll expect you tomorrow, then.
Good-bye.'

'You're all right?' he asked uneasily.

'Yes. Yes, I'm fine.'

'You're alone, I suppose, if Angela's out?'

'Yes.'

'Why don't you go and see the Tanners?'

'I think I'll go to bed. I'm awfully tired.'

'It's only half-past seven. You can't possibly go to bed
at half-past seven.'

'Why not?'

She put down the receiver quickly, before he could
answer. Why not? Why not? Her heart was beating very
fast, her legs trembling. She picked up the musical box and
went back to the kitchen. The tissue paper had blown off
the table in the draught from the open door. She drew the
curtains and poured herself another drink. She thought, as
she sat with her chin in her hand, that she already looked
dissipated. In fact the expression on her face was gentle,
contemplative; she sat patiently, neat in her dark grey suit
and polished shoes; her voice, at first, was hardly audible.

'She hated him—her husband. That isn't quite true, of
course.' There was a long pause. The despair of giving in,
of letting herself go in the emptiness, was almost too much.
She wanted to put her head down on the table and cry,
but the sound of weeping was more frightening than the
sound of words. However silly or dreadful words were, they
were some form of communication, they were human. Perhaps it would be less dangerous if she imagined someone
else was with her. At first this was difficult, because she did

17

not know who to imagine; the listener wavered, was neither a man nor a woman, vanished entirely and was only an empty chair, its white paint glistening in the harsh light. If she did not look at the chair, it was easier.

'Of course,' she said, 'we had to get married. Oh, you didn't know?' She traced the pattern on the formica table-top with her fingernail. Her voice was shy, hesitant. 'I suppose we could have been happy in spite of that. But we never were. I think we hated each other.' Saying these unmentionable things out loud never ceased to horrify her. They were her secrets, battened down so long that they had become almost unrecognisable as the truth. 'Angela was born six months after we were married. She doesn't know, of course. I didn't want to get married. I didn't want Angela. We had to get married. There was nothing else to do.'

She pulled the musical box towards her, holding it between her hands. 'Isn't it pretty? I don't think I shall give it to Jane's baby. She's not old enough to turn the handle, anyway. I'll buy her a doll when I go to Ramsbridge. A teddy bear or something.'

She sighed lightly, as though bored. Her legs had stopped trembling, she felt quite calm. 'I don't know,' she chatted on confidentially, 'why we didn't do anything about it. Well, I do, really. It didn't occur to us. My father said we must get married. No, we didn't even mention it. I wouldn't have known what to do. Rex must have known, but he didn't say anything. We just took it for granted, I suppose. I don't remember. It was nineteen years ago. I had long hair, you know. But really, in pigtails.'

She smiled openly, leaning back in her chair. Her voice was now the perfectly normal, cheerful voice of a woman talking to a friend. 'Shall I have another drink? Oh, it's only my third, the glasses are terribly small. Rex used to be different. Did you know he used to play the guitar? I have a photograph when Julian was a baby—'

She reached for her handbag. Her hand dropped, retreated slowly across the table, fell into her lap. The empty white chair shone under the light; the tap dripped, the door upstairs swung again on its creaking hinges. She sat quite limp, a pretty, tidy woman, terrified to move, the tears spilling soundlessly on to the neat grey costume.

Chapter 3

S HE WOKE, next morning, to fear; then to realisation that the children had gone; then to the sound of water running noisily out of the bathroom basin. She opened her eyes, remembered she was not alone.

'Angela?'

'Hullo.' The voice was muffled, but friendly.

'Did you have a good time?'

An energetic noise, followed, after a moment, by 'Super.'

'What did you do?'

'We had coffee in that scruffy place in King Street. Then we went to the fair.'

'What was it like?'

'Madly expensive.' Angela appeared out of the bathroom drubbing her hair with one of the new bath towels. For some reason she had decided to wash her hair before breakfast. On the rare occasions when she cleaned her room she did it at midnight and, if alone, drank quantities of cocoa.

'Did you have any money?'

'No. Tony paid. Can I borrow your comb?'

She sat down at the dressing-table and began wrestling with the knots in her hair, her face screwed up in anguish.

'I don't know,' Ruth said, 'why you don't have it short.'

'I know,' Angela said between clenched teeth. 'I mean, I know you don't know. Because I should look even more like a lamp-post than I do already. Damn, I've broken it.'

'There's another one in the drawer.'

'I'm awfully sorry.'

'It doesn't matter.'

'I'll get you another one.'

'Oh, darling, it really doesn't matter!' She sat up in bed, her arms round her knees. Something had been forgotten; she groped for it tentatively. 'Didn't you come in very late?'

'Not very.' Withdrawal behind the wet ropes of hair. 'The Tanners' visitors were still there.'

'Oh.' This meant nothing. The Tanners' visitors often stayed till three or four in the morning. Ruth felt she should say so, but found herself saying instead, 'Well, I went to bed fairly early and took a sleeping pill, so perhaps what I heard was the Tanners' visitors leaving.'

'Yes,' Angela said, 'I expect that's what it was.' She pulled at her hair, silent for a few minutes.

'Anyway, I'm glad you had a nice time.'

'After two months,' Angela said, 'of listening to Mike playing "God Save the Queen" on his banjo and Julian grumbling about his wretched meccano, *anything* would seem nice.'

'But just now you said you'd had a marvellous time!'

'Well, I did.' She flung back her hair and hitched the shoulder-straps over her thin shoulders. 'It's just that you seem to think it was so *extraordinary*.'

'Of course I don't think it was extraordinary,' Ruth said slowly. 'What do you mean?'

'Well, I mean, you're terribly understanding and all that,

but you don't seem to realise—' She turned resolutely on the stool, taking a deep breath. Her bony, scrubbed young face was flushed. How dreadfully thin she is, Ruth thought. She ought to have a tonic or something. 'I mean, quite honestly, it's all very well for you living here day after day, after all, it's your home and you've got the boys, and Daddy coming down every weekend and—well, it's your life, isn't it? But you don't seem to realise it's different for me. I'm so lonely sometimes, I could die!'

'But, darling—' They faced each other across the room, both struck with alarm by the outburst, neither of them knowing what to do, how to deal with this small truth that had suddenly exploded in front of them. 'But, darling—you can do exactly as you like! You don't have to come here in the vacations. You don't have to come here at all. I'm sorry you hate it all so much, but—'

'Of course I don't hate it! You don't *understand.*'

'Yes, I do. I do understand.'

'How could you? You were married at my age. I shouldn't think you've ever known a day's loneliness in your life. Oh, I'm sorry.' She covered her face with her long hands. 'I'm sorry,' she wailed. 'Only you don't know the stupid things you do when you're lonely, and there's no one to talk to and nobody cares—'

'Now, don't be silly,' Ruth said roughly. She was out of bed, small, inadequate in her nightgown, her hands firm on the girl's thin arms. 'Stop being so perfectly foolish.' She waited while the quaking subsided, the sobs died to a desolate sniffing. Then she padded across the room and found one of Rex's handkerchiefs. Angela groped for it, still hiding her face with one hand.

'Really,' Ruth said, 'what's come over you?'

'I'm sorry!'

'And *do* stop saying you're sorry!'

She went over to the window, trying to calm herself, to create patience. Now there was an occasion for the truth, she couldn't speak. She could tell Angela everything, but what difference would it make? The effort would be so enormous —what good would it do? Better to take the tall, awkward girl in her arms, pat and kiss and rock the moment away. That was what she wanted, what she was waiting for. It was impossible. The impossibility was painful, a paralysis against all her will, her desire for the child to be happy. She longed to be able to do it, and couldn't. She moved her arms restlessly, rubbed one bare foot against the other, pretended to smother a yawn.

'It's a lovely day. You might take the croquet hoops in before Folkes mows the lawn.'

'Julian left the mallets out. They're all rotting.'

'Look what I got yesterday.'

'What is it?'

'A musical box. Listen.' She turned the handle.

'Really, Mummy, you are a fool.' In spite of herself, Angela laughed, wiping her face with the back of her hand while the other clenched the clean handkerchief. 'What on earth did you get that for?'

'I don't know,' Ruth said, ashamed. 'I thought Jane's baby might like it.'

'She'd break it in five minutes. Poor old Mum, you know you're getting awfully odd.' She blew her nose at last, got up and wandered back to the bathroom. 'I think,' she said, over the sound of running water, 'that you're going to be one of the great English eccentrics.' There were a few moments of splashing and gasping and she came back, drying her face on the other new towel. 'I can just see you in another five years' time, button boots and a picture hat, dr-i-i-fting about the garden in clouds of net or whatever it is.'

'Five years?' Ruth asked, putting the musical box back on the table.

'Ten, then. I'm sorry about all that. I don't know what happened. Shall I make breakfast?' She had fastened herself into the black jeans, dragged on the sweater.

'Yes,' Ruth said. 'Thank you.'

'You aren't upset or anything?'

'Of course not.'

'Would you like boiled or scrambled?'

'Whichever you like. I don't mind.'

'Well, you say.'

'Honestly, darling, I don't mind!' She made a great effort, out of all proportion to the problem. 'Scrambled.'

Angela ran downstairs. Two minutes later the wireless blared out and was turned, considerately, softer.

Chapter 4

SHE DOESN'T KNOW ME, Ruth thought. She's never known me. It's all my fault. 'I shouldn't think you've ever known a day's loneliness in your life.' Did she believe that? Would it make her happier if she knew the truth?

Not the truth, of course. How much of it, then? Last night I . . . No, it would sound too silly. Look, darling, I don't think you understand . . . But why should she? A child wasn't expected to understand its mother. Look, darling, I need your help . . . That was probably better. Relying on her, making her feel needed. You aren't a child any more and I'm terribly worried because—

Well, straight out with it, then. 'I know you think I let you down all the time and that I don't care because I can't comfort you when you're unhappy, but I do care, the fact is that something happens to me, I get frightened. Listen, Angela, I must make you understand.'

Was that straight? It was nothing. Listen, Angela—

'But why should I say this? Perhaps it's not even true.'

She pressed the back of her hand over her mouth. The whisper hung in the quiet, sunny room. She ran downstairs, buttoning the sleeves of her shirt.

Angela was sitting at the kitchen table, her chin in her hands. As Ruth came in she looked up quickly, almost guiltily. Her face was set in the stern, anxious expression of someone who has been deliberately thinking things out and has come to a sad conclusion. She got up and fetched the scrambled eggs from under the grill, served them out and sat down again. There was an ominous silence. Neither of them began to eat.

'Look, Mummy, I—'

'Darling, I—'

They both spoke at once. They both laughed, awkwardly.

'Sorry,' Angela said. 'What were you going to say?'

'Nothing. What were you going to say?'

'I've forgotten. I'm not sure whether I put in any salt.'

They began to eat. The wireless, subdued, yelled passionate love songs for housewives in Hull.

'Has the post come?'

'Yes. Only a couple of bills.'

'It seems,' Ruth said tentatively, 'funny without the children. Only yesterday morning Mike was making all that fuss about the toast.'

'It seems pure bliss to me.'

'Does it? Yes, well, I suppose it would. I can't get used to it, somehow.'

'Well,' Angela said, pushing her plate away and sighing deeply, 'I suppose that's natural.'

'I suppose so.'

Angela began drawing on the tablecloth with her knife. She scored two deep lines, then crossed them with two more.

'I must be getting odd,' Ruth blurted out desperately, 'I talk to myself all the time.'

'Mm. I've noticed. Tony's father's an architect. He designed something or other for the Festival of Britain.'

'Oh,' Ruth said, 'did he?'

'Perhaps you saw it. It was called the Hall of Tomorrow or something.'

'No,' Ruth said. 'I don't think I saw it.'

'Well, apparently he's famous.'

'Darling, do stop cutting up the tablecloth. You're as bad as Julian.'

'I'm sorry.' She threw the knife down and pulled out the *New Statesman* from under the pile of newspapers.

'I thought Daddy said you were to cancel that.'

'He didn't. He said if I wanted it I was to pay for it myself. Jolly tolerant of him.' She leafed through it hopelessly. 'Considering it's read by all the most intelligent people in the country.'

'I think I shall have to go to the doctor,' Ruth said in a flat, informative voice.

'Why don't you get him to come out? It's such a bore, waiting in that surgery.' She became suddenly alert, and then as suddenly casual, 'Do you think this is true?'

'What?' Ruth asked wearily.

'The Knaus-Ogino Discovery.'

'What on earth is it?'

' "The brilliant discoveries of Professor Hermann Knaus and Dr. Kyasaku Ogino—" '

'No,' Ruth said. 'It's not true.'

'You don't even know what it is. ". . . have established as a scientific fact that a woman can conceive only on certain days of the month and no others. Calculating these fertile days accurately, depending as they do on so many variables, has always meant working out complicated sums each month —if one knew how." '

'If,' Ruth said, 'indeed.'

'Oh, do listen. "Now," it says, "with the aid of a specially designed, brilliant little Swiss precision calculator, the fertile days are shown in advance for each month and any healthy woman can plan her family naturally, confidently and in private." Do you think it's true?'

'I don't know,' Ruth said. 'I suppose it might be. It's probably done by all the most intelligent people in the country.'

'But would you use a thing like that?'

'No. I don't know. Perhaps.'

Angela's eyes flickered up, took in her mother, quick, momentarily embarrassed. 'Well, anyway, it says it excludes any possibility of mathematical error and automatically takes into consideration irregularities of—'

'Yes,' Ruth said. 'You could probably do the whole thing by radar—if you knew how. Shall we wash up?'

Slowly, Angela closed the paper. 'I'm sorry,' she said. 'I only wondered if it was true.'

'How do I know?'

'Yes, but—'

'And in any case,' Ruth heard herself saying, wilfully stupid, 'I think it's frightful to have advertisements like that—for children to read. I'll wash. You dry.'

'Isn't Mrs. Wilson coming?'

'There'll be quite enough for her to do. Daddy's bringing the Craxtons for the weekend.'

'Oh, God. How ghastly. How absolutely ghastly.'

Ruth said nothing. The plates and cups and saucers piled up on the draining-board. At last Angela moved and began,

28

laboriously, to dry them. She seemed absurdly upset. The battle she was having with herself was almost audible, charging the air with incomprehensible and distant cries.

At last, in a high, polite voice she asked: 'Why do you have to go to the doctor? Aren't you well?'

'I'm fine,' Ruth said. She let the water out of the sink and dried her hands on her apron. 'Do you like Tony?'

'Yes. He's all right.'

They separated, haughty and distressed; both, in a curious way, snatched back from danger.

Chapter 5

W HAT ON EARTH'S THIS?' Rex paused in his weekly inspection of the bedroom, picked up the musical box and glared at it suspiciously. He was still fully dressed and had not yet finished his cigar. He was restless because Jill Craxton had bundled, as she would say, her husband off to bed and he couldn't stay alone downstairs. He had no intention, obviously, of sleeping.

'It's a musical box,' Ruth said, turning over away from the light.

'What for?'

'It's not for anything. You turn the handle. It plays a tune.'

Her eyes firmly closed, she heard the plaintive, sweet dirge tinkling like glass prisms touching in the wind.

'You mean to say that you actually bought this thing?'

'Yes.'

'How much did it cost?'

'I don't remember. I'm not sure.'

From the short, exasperated sigh she knew that he had put it back on the table and, shrugging his shoulders, resumed his walk. Now he was inspecting her dressing-table. Now he was looking at himself in the mirror, stroking the rough skin under his chin with the tips of his fingers. She opened her eyes. That was exactly what he was doing. She shut them again, afraid, in the mirror, to be seen awake.

'Jill's in very good form,' he said. 'I think she's the funniest woman I know.'

Obediently, her mouth twitched into a little grimace of mirth. 'Yes,' she murmured.

'When she told that story about the lavatory attendant at the Tower Ballroom I thought she'd split her dress open. Not very funny really, but it's good to see such zest. Everyone's so bloody sensitive, it bores you stiff.'

She turned on her back, locking her arms behind her head.

'Do you meet a lot of sensitive people?'

'Too many.' He looked at her suspiciously. 'Was that a joke?'

'No. What do you mean?'

'I thought,' he said angrily, 'you might have made a joke. People do make jokes like that, you know.'

'Oh,' she said. 'I didn't think of it.'

He moved the cigar butt round his big, moist lips and picked up her hairbrush, absently brushing his hair.

'Heard from the boys yet?' he asked.

'No. They only went yesterday.'

'Oh, yes. I suppose they did. Angela seems in a very bad temper.'

'I think,' she said, reckless with weariness, 'that she's bored.'

'Bored? Why on earth should she be bored?'

'I suppose she finds it dull here.'

'Dull? Here? What on earth do you mean?'

'I don't,' she said wildly, 'mean anything on earth. I mean she finds it dull here. She's lonely. That's all.'

'But why on—why in the world should she be lonely?'

'Oh, Rex.' She twisted her head once on the pillow. 'I don't *know*. Why not ask her?'

'I certainly will. Good God, there aren't many girls with her advantages. Why doesn't she join the tennis club?'

'She doesn't like tennis.'

'Well, what *does* she like? Why doesn't she go out with some of these brilliant left-wing Teddy Boys we hear so much about?'

'Do you?'

'Do I what? Why do you have to mumble all the time?'

'Hear so much about them. I don't. Anyway, she did go out last night. I told you.'

'It doesn't seem to have done her much good.'

He dropped the dead, wet butt of the cigar into the ash-tray and bent to unlace his shoes. It was an effort. He was forty-five and putting on a lot of weight. In his expensive clothes he still managed to look suave and tidy, to emanate the bitter-sweet smell of money and after-shave. But even in front of Ruth, he would hurry into his pyjamas. She turned on her side again, pushing her face into the pillow.

'Anyway,' he said, when the shoes were off, 'who was this boy? What?'

'I don't know. His father's an architect.'

'What's his name?'

'Tony.'

'No, I mean his father's name!'

'I don't know,' she said softly into the pillow. 'I don't know.'

'Don't you know anything?'

She shook her head. Against the moist, stifling softness her face was screwed into an exaggerated expression of anguish, teeth bared and clenched, eyes screwed tight, muscles rigid. She held her breath, prolonging the terrible, secret contortion.

'You're supposed to be her mother, aren't you? How do you know what goes on with these boys she goes out with?' He was righteous; conviction gave a firm, clear ring to his voice. 'For all you know she spent the evening in the Red Lion. In bed. What?'

'She didn't. She had some coffee with him and went to the fair.'

'And I suppose nothing can happen at fairs?'

She made a little convulsive movement, hunching herself in the bed.

'You should know,' he said. 'And it's not going to happen to any daughter of mine. It's your responsibility. You're the woman. If anything happens to Angela, you'll be entirely to blame. And as far as I'm concerned, you can be sure of one thing. I'd turn her out.'

She had read somewhere that long ago people believed that the purpose of the brain was to drop cool vapours on to the heart, cooling its passions. This seemed to happen to her now. She felt immediately calm. Her face relaxed into its normal, gentle, slightly enquiring expression. Her fingers loosened on the pillow. She turned and sat up, vaguely pushing back her hair.

'Out of where?'

'Certainly out of this house she finds so exceedingly dull.' He wrenched off his collar, heaved himself out of his braces.

'You don't mean it,' she said, as though comforting him.

'Of course I mean it." He turned on her furiously. 'Why will you always insist I don't mean things? I mean what I say and I say—'

She smiled, joining in. 'What you think.'

'Well, I do. Good God, I know what I think. Now take that argument at dinner tonight.'

'Oh—' She lay back on the pillows.

'Well, what about it?'

'Angela didn't agree with you. That's all.'

'Well, *why* didn't she agree with me? I was right, wasn't I?'

'I—'

'Go on. Was I right or not?'

'I—I don't know.'

'Christ!' he said. 'You don't know. What's the matter with you? Why don't you know?'

She took a deep breath. 'All right, then. I think you were wrong. But I don't think you meant it, because,' she rushed over his furious interruption, 'if you thought about it, you couldn't mean it. I think you just said it because you knew Angela wouldn't like it. You want to hurt her. You don't want her to agree with you. You just want to hurt her.'

They were both equally amazed. She stared at him, her mouth open. He struggled with speech as though it were strangling him.

'Don't,' she whispered. 'Please. There's no point in it.'

'No point in it!' He floundered hopelessly. 'My God, what are you? Playing with toys—' He picked up the musical box.

'Please don't break it, Rex.'

'How much work do you think I had to do to buy this thing? How much bloody work did I do?'

'Let's go to sleep. The Craxtons will hear you. Let's go to sleep. Please.' 1059927

'Sleep!' But he put the musical box down and lowered his voice. 'That's about it. Sleep. Did it ever occur to you there was any reason for going to bed except to go to sleep?'

She lay down, pulling the sheet up to her chin.

'Well? Did it?'

'I don't know,' she said.

'You don't know!' He stumped off to the bathroom. She listened, remotely, to the furious sound of scrubbing, spitting, and running water. 'It's a good thing,' he said, switching off the bathroom light and walking heavily back across the room, 'that there are some normal women in the world. It's a damned good thing, that's all I can say.'

'Yes,' she said. 'It is.'

He threw himself into bed, sweeping the bedclothes round him and lying angrily with his back to her. She switched off the light. Such anger, such fury—and all for what? To make a little noise, to agitate a few moments and pretend it mattered. She thought of Angela, working alone in her room; of her sons, strangers in some silent dormitory, their gum lodged on the bedrail, twitching and snapping in their sleep like small dogs. These three were real. They were, in their ability to hope, to change, to choose between right and wrong, grown up. For Rex and herself there was no longer any hope or possibility of change; there was no longer any choice to be made. They lay, fully grown, capable of every crime and every greatness, paralysed by triviality.

We are two lonely people, she thought, who might at least comfort each other in the dark. The long, rhythmical sound of Rex's snoring began. She turned over carefully, blocking her ears and stepping, like a nervous swimmer, into sleep.

Chapter 6

HE VILLAGE, on a Sunday morning, is
dead. No road passes through it. There is no work to do.
The village has been stifled in this valley for five hundred
years. It breeds gardeners and charwomen for the Common,
farm-hands for the Rackworth estate. On Sunday there is
nothing in the village but the pealing of church bells, the
energy of hens.

Above the village, but below the Common, lies the vast,
aimless pile of flint and lead known as Rackworth House.
Ralph Rackworth works at his desk, irritated by the bells.
He has equipped his tenants with contemporary light fit-
tings and bidets. He has given the tenant farmers strip-
lighting in the cowsheds and walkie-talkie telephones so
that the farm-hands, jolting up and down the gentle hills
on their clean orange tractors, can pass the time of day.
The medieval bells discourage him.

A tall, murmuring man in rimless glasses, he has his
clothes made for him by a secret tailor: corduroy trousers
so flat across his flat hips that a matchbox in the pocket
would look obscene; great leather jackets lined with fur,
and sombre shirts which give him the look of an ageing

penitent. He plays classic jazz with great brilliance on the Rackworth Broadwood, his shaven, greying head bent rigid over the wandering hands. He has turned his own wing of the house into a desert of subfusc carpeting, a void forever moaning and booming with music. His parents, who are old and failing, creep about their part of the house in plastic macintoshes and retire each night to lie on high, canopied beds like tombs, their little claws peaceably folded, their small faces caved in with sleep. They are the only ones to obey the bells. They know where, and how deep, they will be buried when they die.

Sunday morning on the Common has a distinction of its own. The people who live on the Common are wealthy. They need high-powered cars to reach their otherwise inaccessible homes and they need high-powered homes to make the journey worth while. Like a class in school, they are all much the same age, wear the same sort of clothes and specialise, with only slightly varying degrees of success, in the subject of money. Every week contains at least two clear days of leisure, but on Sunday they rest. Sunday is a recurrent observance that has nothing to do with God and yet contains, in its prolonged silences, the distant pealing of bells, the wafts of roast mutton across the undisturbed bracken, the lazy spirals of smoke, a nostalgic piety; a sense, as in remembering old Sundays and old summers, of lassitude and loss.

Except for the occasional lonely child, too young to be sent to school, no one stirs until midday. The mutton is roasted, the apple pies prepared by capable cooks, German or Swiss or Norwegian, who are saving up enough money to travel round the world. Later in the day they will mount their bicycles and pedal in organised groups to each other's houses where they will eat tinned frankfurters and potato salad, smoke Turkish cigarettes and discuss the advantages of India over Brazil. Most of them call their employers by their Christian names and spend much of the day in a state of slight and agreeable intoxication owing to the glasses of sherry continually pressed on them to keep them happy.

At noon, all over the Common like a series of elaborate cuckoo-clocks, the various front doors open and the stock-brokers and dentists, company directors and chartered accountants, directors of advertising agencies and manufac-turers of plastic, step out on to their baize-green grass and reverently breathe the Sunday air. The literary agent, the film director and the playwright, their tenure less secure, emerge a few minutes later, hurriedly and guiltily inspect-ing the gravel for weeds while nobody is looking. High yew hedges, roosters and domes of privet, sometimes an acre of wild land, separate these houses from each other, and yet an aerial view would show a solitary figure in each garden, the same flash of doggy yellow or hunting pink, the same white flag of newspaper carelessly folded after breakfast; and, in a little while, the same tiny wives, popping out like an afterthought into the sun.

The wives have less resemblance to each other than the men. They conform to a certain standard of dress, they run their houses along the same lines, bring their children up in the same way; all prefer coffee to tea, all drive cars, play bridge, own at least one valuable piece of jewellery and are moderately good-looking. That is all that can be seen. But it isn't all.

The relationships between the men are based on an understanding of success. Admiration is general, affection not uncommon. Even pity is known. The women have no such understanding. Like little icebergs, each keeps a bright and shining face above water; below the surface, submerged in fathoms of leisure, each keeps her own isolated personality. Some are happy, some poisoned with boredom; some drink too much and some, below the demarcation line, are slightly crazy; some love their husbands and some are dying from lack of love; a few have talent, as useless to them as a paralysed limb. Their friendships, appearing frank and sunny, are febrile and short-lived, turning quickly to malice. Combined, their energy could start a revolution, power half of Southern England, drive an atomic plant. It is all directed towards the effortless task of living on the Common. There are times, towards the middle of the school term, when the quiet air seems charged, ready to spit lightning; when it is dangerous to touch a shrilling telephone and a coffee cup may explode without reason.

There is, however, no sign of this as, dressed for Sunday in tight checked pants and cashmere sweaters, the wives join their husbands in the bronze and gold September gardens. A few, the hosts for this morning, stay where they are. Some take their dogs and set out slowly, couples meeting and greeting on the winding, spongy paths, sometimes going on together, sometimes parting. Those who live on the periphery of the Common get out their cars and bowl like black, glinting marbles along the unfenced roads. There is not one heretic; not one Commoner who, on this mellow Sunday morning, does not taste the sweet comfort of sherry, the content of a cheese straw.

Chapter 7

RUTH SAW THE TANNERS arriving as she stood by Angela's bedroom window. They had brought their weekend guests. Richard, small, dapper, wearing a gabardine cap, walked in front with a blonde girl whose hands, hanging limply from bent elbows, swung from side to side like pendulums. Behind them was a tall, thin man in Prince of Wales check who leaned confidentially towards Jane and the inevitable pram. Jane, never taking her eyes off the heaving blankets, nodded emphatically. They rounded the corner of the house.

'They've arrived,' Ruth said.

'Who?'

'The Tanners and the people who are staying for the weekend.'

'Oh.' Angela looked up for a moment from the floor where, stretched on her stomach like a scrawled black line, she was reputedly working. 'Of course. I can hear that brat crying.'

'Do come down. It looks so rude. Everyone knows you're here. They think you're superior.'

'Honestly, why should I come down and be bored to death by that dreary lot? The Craxtons are bad enough. I thought I should *die* last night.'

'I must go. I wish you'd come.'

'No, thanks.' She squinted up as Ruth, dragging and reluctant as a child, went to the door. 'Give them all my fondest love.'

Ruth walked slowly along the corridor. At the end of the corridor a large window opened above the garden. Jane Tanner was wheeling her child smartly backwards and forwards across the lawn like an obedient, though curiously encumbered sentry. She was the one Common wife for whom Ruth felt a warm, if often confused, affection. Jane seldom understood anything anyone said to her, being entirely obsessed with the sounds of wind, grief, fury or contentment which had just emerged, or were emerging, or were about to emerge from the cot or pram. She lived in a state of perpetual danger, frantic with the knowledge that it was possible for a child to drown in two inches of water, that cats habitually suffocated babies by jumping into their prams, that nightdresses meant certain death and every other man was a sexual maniac. In the surface of life, which they shared, Ruth felt comparatively calm and unthreatened.

'Jane?'

Jane did not slacken pace for a moment. She glanced up, saw Ruth leaning out of the window, beat the air for silence, pointed at the pram, shrugged her shoulders hopelessly and wheeled round by the mulberry tree. The child, dizzy with speed, was blacking out. 'In a minute,' she mouthed, jabbing a finger towards the house. Ruth nodded and went, stair by stair, trailing her hand on the banisters, towards the sitting-room.

When the Tanners first came, she had been alarmed by them. Jane had been Tanner's secretary for five years before she married him and was considered, to begin with, a misfit. Even her appearance, the one-third above the surface, had been discouraging—urban, brisk and intelligent. Unlike other wives, she knew exactly where the money came from and how. She knew the kind of life Richard led between Monday and Friday, where he hung his hat, in which drawer he kept the magnesia tablets and that he had accumulated, at one time, a small library of pornographic books in the cupboard next to the filing cabinet. There had been no time to find out whether this knowledge would have proved a good or a bad thing. She immediately became pregnant.

What happened to her during the six hours of labour nobody ever knew. Something snapped or something fell into place, or her brain, under pressure, tossed about like the coloured pieces in a kaleidoscope, settled in an entirely different pattern. Whatever it was, when she came out of the nursing home she was fat, cosy, middle-aged and had already formed the habit of breaking, in the middle of a sentence, into an irrelevant chant, as though possessed by some voodoo: 'Duzzy-wuzzy, cosy-wozy, woops-a-daisy, there's my popsy-wopsy, tiny belch for Mumsy-wumsy?' There was nothing to be done about it. Jane, the wives said with satisfaction, had fulfilled herself.

Her marriage, although she didn't realise it, had been killed on the spot. She refused, on dimly remembered psychological grounds, to have a nurse for the child, but employed a sad little Swiss to operate the battery of machines that hummed and thundered in the kitchen. She believed, rather pathetically, that she 'kept up with things,' but this consisted in asking an occasional failure to the house in order to disrupt what would otherwise have been, to her husband, a tolerable atmosphere of success. Her private fantasy, indulged in during the brief periods when the child was allowed to go to sleep, was that she held on the Common a kind of salon, or refuge for the unappreciated. Escaping from the mad whirl of London, radio actors and male fashion models, slogan writers who should have been poets and poets who were, inexplicably, radio actors, could find a serene haven. Since she never went up to London these lost sheep were becoming increasingly difficult to find. They seldom, after being in close contact with Baby for two days, came again.

This weekend the victims were a gaunt young man called Herb and his friend, Maxine. Both, she had explained hurriedly to Ruth on the telephone, were interested in something called Basic Theatre. She did not say that she had only met Herb once, at a party three years ago, when he had been playing the mercifully brief part of a subaltern going mad in the trenches in the 1914 war. She had been struck, she vaguely remembered, by the fact that he had read three books on Mental Disorder before attempting this task and that towards the end of the party he had suddenly shouted, 'I can't stand it! I can't stand it!' and bolted heroically out of the room. She had been secretly relieved that he seemed to remember who she was, not realising that suddenly presented with a free weekend this hardly mattered. In fact he hadn't the faintest idea who she was. Who, as Maxine had asked him, cared?

Chapter 8

IT'S A WONDERFUL PLACE you have here, Mrs. Whiting.'

'Thank you.'

'You know, these country weekends of yours just about slay me. The pace is terrific.'

'They don't have country weekends in Leicester,' Maxine breathed. 'Herb comes from Leicester, you know. You might think he came from the States, but he doesn't. He comes from Leicester.'

'Well,' Craxton said heartily, 'that's clear enough.'

Everyone laughed. Maxine turned slowly back to Rex, devoting herself to him, her face more grave than any grave face, her voice softer than anyone speaking softly. She was a very sensitive girl and deeply interested in the theatre. She had already confided that her hair was naturally blonde, but that she had often thought of dyeing it so that people would take her more seriously.

'Hell,' Herb said, 'has no fury like a girl who has to pay her own rent.' He was quarreling with Maxine. He gazed penetratingly at Ruth through half-closed eyes. 'Were you ever in Leicester, Mrs. Whiting?'

'No,' Ruth said. 'No, I don't think so.'

'Who is this man?' Jill Craxton demanded, easing Ruth out of the way. 'He has a wicked twinkle in his eye.'

'Hullo, gorgeous,' Richard Tanner said gloomily. 'Come and talk to me. Boys gone off to school yet?'

'Yes, they went on Thursday. How are you, Richard?'

'How do I look?'

Automatically she switched on the sweet, skittish look reserved by the wives for each other's husbands. 'Poorly,' she said. 'Yes, poorly.'

'Dear Ruth, if only you knew——'

Everyone was distracted by the arrival of the Johnsons with their Labrador, an eager animal which raced round the room three times, knocking over various small pieces of furniture and panting in an affected way until it was given a bowl of water, which it immediately stepped in. The Johnsons meanwhile made hopeless gestures of slapping their thighs, snapping their fingers and lunging clumsily about in its wake.

'Isn't he sweet?' Maxine whispered ecstatically. 'I have such a very real affection for dogs. They seem to me to be more *loving* than people, somehow. Do you think that's very eccentric of me, Mr. Whiting?'

'I like dogs myself,' Rex said. 'Unfortunately we can't have one.'

'But why ever not, Mr. Whiting?'

'My wife doesn't care for them, and since she's alone here all the week it doesn't seem worth it.'

'But it would be such company for her, Mr. Whiting!'

'She doesn't care for company.'

The Wilmington-Smiths burst in on a wail of disaster.

'Darling, I'm sorry we're so late but what *do* you think? Edelgard's given notice—on a Sunday, can you imagine, and just in the *middle* of everything! I could die, I really could die!'

The women gathered round, magnetised by the crisis.

'She says she wants to go to Johannesburg—Ruth, dear, could I have a large gin?—but, as I pointed out to her, you can't just *go* to Johannesburg like that, you need tickets and visas and heaven knows what. But she said she had it all arranged, she was going for a walking tour in the Black Forest first. Can you imagine such selfishness? Thank you so much, darling, I really need it. She says she hasn't had a holiday for three months—well, I ask you, who has? I could really cry. In fact I did cry, didn't I, John?'

'So did she,' her husband said uncomfortably. 'I never heard such a row.'

'Well, what am I going to *do?* Of course it's so easy for you, darling, you have a grown-up daughter—'

Now the party was complete. Out on the lawn, exhausted and almost in tears, Jane was wheeling the child round the mulberry tree for the fiftieth time. In the sitting-room the sherry went quickly to their heads, they talked more loudly, the waves of laughter gathered momentum, broke and receded and gathered again; the Labrador lapped sherry out of forgotten glasses.

'I met Angela the other day,' Ruth heard herself say, in a vague and wondering voice, 'rushing past on the back of someone's Vespa—'

Chapter 9

VESPA? WHOSE VESPA?'

'I haven't the faintest idea. Some young man from Oxford, I imagine. You know what they're like—' The reproduction was faultless: a slight pause, a breath of indulgence, 'They never tell one a thing.'

'Oh, Mrs. Whiting—do you mean to say you really have a grown-up daughter?'

'She's eighteen,' Rex said.

'Isn't that amazing? Only five years younger than me, and I wouldn't have thought you were a day over thirty!'

'It was a *News of the World* case,' Richard said, 'at the time.'

'You're not serious, Mr. Tanner? It wasn't *really?*'

Richard yawned. After a night in the company of Baby, he couldn't be bothered with Maxine.

'Oh, I see. You're only joking.' Maxine turned from him coldly. 'I do think it must be wonderful to have a young mother, I mean a mother who looks young. Do you find you have a great understanding?'

'Well—' Ruth said.

'A book I was reading the other day said that the mother-daughter relationship was much more difficult than the father-son relationship. Although personally,' her eyes widened and brightened as she remembered this fascinating, though apparently irrelevant facet of her personality, 'I rather like Teddy Boys.'

'I'm not surprised,' Betty Johnson murmured.

The Johnsons lived in a row of converted cottages: that is, although they lived in all the cottages, they were not exactly Commoners. Robert's car, although large and powerful, was not new. He was some years younger than his wife and came home every night. He was known as poor Robert. He was terrified of women in case they should smile at him, touch him, put their legs or breasts where he couldn't avoid seeing them. Most of the time he looked at the floor.

What with watching Robert to see if he looked at Maxine and watching Maxine in case she smiled at Robert and trying to control the dog and drinking, in the stress of it all, too much sherry, Betty Johnson felt abandoned and capable of murder.

'I dare say,' she said, 'you have a lot in common.'

The others sat to attention, glowed with good humour as though, with one accord, they had caught the rays of a flashing arctic sun.

'I think it's quite terrifying,' someone babbled, 'when one thinks of one's children growing up, particularly girls. I mean, how does one prevent the most ghastly things happening to them?'

'One doesn't,' Jill Craxton said. 'They all get married, don't they?'

'Well, one hopes so.'

'But suppose they start popping into bed with all and sundry *before?*'

'Obvious,' Rex said. 'Just tell them not to.'

'Oh, I agree,' Maxine breathed. 'I don't think all this freedom is good for a girl. I mean, it doesn't make you happy, does it? I mean, all that sort of thing is sacred, really. I'm sure you all think I'm very old-fashioned.' She met, with candour, the stares of amazement. 'I just think about things,' she explained modestly, 'it's funny, but I just can't help it. I think nearly all the time.'

Maxine's interruptions were like small landslides on a familiar path. The women stepped round them, pretending they weren't there; the men either observed them with interest or thankfully gave up the conversation altogether.

'You can't keep 'em locked up,' John Wilmington-Smith said. This seemed to strike him as humorous and he laughed savagely, his long, heavily moustached mouth opening and shutting abruptly. 'We don't live in the Dark Ages, you know.'

'No,' Maxine said, 'that's what I think, but—'

'Oh, for God's sake, what's all the fuss about?' Rex heaved himself out of his chair and went for the decanter. 'Girls should stay virgins until they marry. It's as simple as that. What?'

'But how?' Jill Craxton asked. 'That's all we want to know, dear. How?'

Jane Tanner crept through the french windows, shut them with exaggerated caution and tiptoed across the room. She sank, exhausted, on the sofa.

'She's asleep,' she whispered. 'With the most menacing smile on her face you ever saw.'

'Isn't she rather old,' Betty Johnson asked sharply, 'to be sleeping in a pram?'

'Is there any reason,' Jane enquired, bitterly civil, 'why she shouldn't sleep in a pram? Is there any law?'

Betty flushed, conscious of hostility. 'I thought it was rather unusual. Naturally, I don't know about children.'

'No,' Jane said. She smiled brilliantly at Jill Craxton. 'Have you any idea why we do it? I'm wearing myself out for that monstrous child. She won't sleep at night, the only thing that sends her off is perpetual motion. What can I do?'

Somebody undoubtedly said, 'Drown her.' It might have been Richard.

Jane's face hardened slightly. 'I'm sure,' she said deliberately, 'she's dreaming of stretching me on the rack or putting lighted matches under my fingernails. Robert, love, what a perfectly gorgeous tie!'

Robert Johnson blushed and began picking up small crumbs from the carpet.

'It is rather nice, isn't it?' Betty said. 'I got it in Simpsons last time I was up in town.'

They all brightened again.

'You don't know,' Maxine said, 'how exciting it is to hear people really having a conversation. I mean, really intelligent people. I do miss it so in London.'

'Did I interrupt a conversation?' Jane asked with horror. 'What about?'

They all found it hard to remember. Domestic help? Children? Dogs? Golf?

'Well,' Maxine said, 'it was about sex, really.'

They all smiled at her gratefully, except for Betty Johnson who said, 'Nonsense,' and began to pull on her gloves. Nobody took any notice of her, and Rex poured her husband another drink.

'We were just wondering,' Jill Craxton said, 'how we save our daughters from a fate worse than death. Rex says you just lock them up and send them pure to the altar. Mine's only eight, but I must say I often wonder.'

'Well, mine's only two,' Jane said briskly, 'and I don't wonder at all. I shall see that she knows everything, always, and when she's a reasonable age—'

'Ha, ha.' John Wilmington-Smith erupted again. 'But what's a reasonable age? Eh?'

'It all depends on the child. Before she goes to the University, naturally.'

'Well, Mrs. Tanner!' Maxine howled softly. 'I think you're inhuman, really I do. When I think of that sweet little baby—well really, I could cry. Wouldn't you like to see her married all in white, with the organ and bridesmaids and everything? And her picture in the paper?'

'What on earth's that got to do with it?' Jane asked. 'She can be married in bottle green for all I care.'

'Oh, for God's sake, Jane,' Rex said. 'You know perfectly well what Miss—'

'O'Donovan,' Maxine murmured.

'What Miss O'Donovan means. What's Dick got to say to all this, that's what I'd like to know? What?'

Richard Tanner yawned loudly. 'Oh, the hell with it. We'll probably all be dead by then, anyway. Ruth's the only person who's concerned by all this, as far as I can see. Why not ask *her*?'

They all turned towards Ruth. She parted her lips and took a breath. What did she think? That Jane was right; and yet, that Jane was wrong. That it was all terribly important; that it didn't matter, was no more than the

52

wandering of voices in a dead Sunday. That her opinion was
... that she had done ... that she intended—

'She doesn't know,' Rex said. 'That's the wonderful thing
about Ruth. She acts by instinct.'

'But that is so wonderful. Don't you think so? Because
a mother's instinct is always so right and I'm sure,' Maxine
smiled angelically, 'Mrs. Whiting is a wonderful mother.
I do wish I could meet your daughter, Mrs. Whiting. I'm
sure we'd get on *terribly* well.'

'I'm sorry,' Ruth said. 'She's working.' She felt defeated
and beaten and old. Somewhere outside this smoky room
with its crumbs and dying flowers, the sprightly clothes
packed with ageing bodies, the intimacy and malice, was the
world. Ships were moving round it, dinghies across bays,
canoes up rivers; Negroes were sitting down to lunch and
soldiers lying in ditches, giraffes eating the tops of trees.
Were they perhaps all dead, without knowing it?

'Can you hear her?'

'Hear her? Hear who?'

'I thought you must have heard Baby crying.'

'No. No, I didn't hear her.'

'Oh. Well, come on, all. Time for din-din.'

Maxine slithered out of her chair and Herb, who had
been trying to explain himself to Craxton and felt once more
a man among men, shook Ruth's hand warmly.

'A wonderful party,' he said. 'It's a real home you have
here.'

'Thank you,' Ruth said absently.

'I'm told you have an eighteen-year-old daughter. They
must be pulling my leg.'

'Good-bye,' Ruth said.

'Only five years younger than me,' Maxine breathed, clinging to Rex's hand. 'Can you believe it?'

Ruth stood in the doorway and watched the slow, unsteady procession wandering down the gravel drive. It was headed by the Johnsons, not speaking, the Labrador darting and nosing round them; then the Wilmington-Smiths, flanking Maxine, who needed more room to walk than they were giving her; then Herb and Jane; and finally Richard, his cap pulled well down over his eyes, his feet dragging, pushing the gleaming pram, from which seeped a thin scream of protest.

Will nothing ever happen to us, she wondered. Will this really go on forever? Is it possible that nothing will ever change?

Chapter 10

OH GOD—Angela's only exclamation of despair—will nothing ever happen, nothing, nothing? Her room at home became, towards the end of the vacation, a kind of intolerable refuge. She hated it, and only left it for meals. With the door shut, the wireless blaring, the windows steamed over, she could indulge in boredom, despair, absolute idleness. Her mother hurried along the corridor outside, up and down stairs, in and out of empty rooms like a cat in search of its kittens. The Hoover moaned, the telephone rang, tradesmen banged on the back door. Angela lay on the floor in front of the electric fire, her head on her arms, staring at the hard tufts of the rug, smelling dust.

Her chief occupation was writing to Tony. '*I wrote to you this morning, so there isn't really anything to tell you—*' There wasn't. She sucked the end of her fountain pen, looking hopelessly up and round the room. '*Everything seems a million miles away when I'm here and I just can't imagine that this time next week we'll be back in Oxford—*' what a pointless thing to say—'*and I'll be able to talk to you instead of just writing.*' Not even true. I never talk to him. I just listen. '*When you come on Sunday,*' she went on quickly, '*I suppose you'll think this is just an ordinary house and you won't believe anything I've told you, so in a way I rather dread you coming. Mummy is very worried about my* luggage. *She says how can I get all my luggage on a Vespa, but whether this is because she disapproves of you coming to fetch me I don't know. Anyhow I don't have any luggage, so don't worry. Because you are the first boy friend of mine she's ever seen I think she's in a tizz—anyway, she's asked me twice if you like cucumber sandwiches, so you'd better. She doesn't know anything about us and she's just not interested, which is just as well, since she wouldn't understand a thing. I think she is getting worse and sometimes I feel quite* desperate *with her, because it's awful having no one to depend on over the slightest thing—and of course that's what wrong with me and you're quite right when you say I suffer from insecurity—*'

She sighed bitterly. Oh, she thought, how I bore myself. What does he care about all this, and anyway I've said it a hundred times before. But she had to pretend he cared. They were in love, weren't they? '*You're the only person I've ever cared for,*' she lied, stubborn, '*and I suppose you're the only person I've ever trusted, too. When I'm with you I feel that everything's* certain, *you're the only* real *person in the world, when I say that you're the first person I've ever loved I don't just mean as far as sex is concerned— although that's true—but right back to the beginning of my life—*'

She wrote quickly now, covering page after page. He was nearer to her than he had ever been, clasped in her thin, hesitant arms. She had achieved, by imagination, the impossible. She had made him indistinguishable from herself.

He was a small young man with a long nose and hair cut like a Roman centurion's. He called Rex 'sir' and smoked a pipe. He did not look at Angela, or, except when absolutely necessary, speak to her.

'One thing I missed when I was overseas,' he said, as Ruth passed him the last cucumber sandwich, 'tea. There's nothing like it. I'm something of a tea-taster, actually. This, of course, is Earl Grey.'

'Angela,' Ruth said, 'give him another cup.'

'I can always tell. My mother, now, has Twinings' Lapsang Su Chong. The other day they sent a packet of Peking Chu Fin by mistake. No one noticed it except me.'

'Well,' Ruth said, 'how extraordinary.'

'Yes, it is really.'

'How long were you—overseas?'

'Two years. National Service. The happiest days of my life. I'm just filling in time till the next war, actually. I'm a complete militarist.'

'Why?' Rex asked, with interest.

'Well, sir, I just love the life. In the next war I intend to be a colonel. I shall wear jeans and an American battledress jacket and a bright yellow scarf and a bull terrier.'

'He means,' Angela said, 'he will lead the dog about. Like a mascot.'

'But won't it be difficult if you go abroad?' Ruth asked. 'I mean, quarantine and so on?'

'Not at all.'

'The next war,' Rex said, 'won't give you much time for that sort of thing.'

'Well, actually, sir, I don't agree. I think all this talk of the H-bomb and so on is a lot of nonsense, frankly. It's much more likely that we shall go back to the old trench warfare.

I wouldn't be surprised if they didn't revive the cavalry, actually. Political wars are a thing of the past. All people want a war for now is to blow off steam. Nobody used gas in the last war, did they? But they did in 1914.'

'In the last war,' Rex said with remarkable patience, 'they used the atom bomb.'

'Exactly. So they won't use it in the next one. All these things are just a flash in the pan, really. The only point in a war is to give people something to do, as far as I can see. Of course, I realise it's a pretty revolutionary point of view.'

'Would you like some more tea?' Ruth asked.

'No, thanks. Do you mind a pipe?'

'Not a bit. And what are you reading at Oxford?'

'English. But as I say, it's just filling in the time, really.'

'And what are you going to do—if there isn't another war, I mean?'

'God knows.' He dropped his dead match into the ashtray held out by Angela. 'I suppose there's always the British Council. Actually, I wouldn't mind a job on the Stock Exchange.'

'I hear your father's an architect?' Rex asked. It was obvious that he was impressed by Tony.

'Yes. He's a frightful old Bolshie, but we get on pretty well. We're always arguing, of course.'

'So are we,' Angela said, blushing.

'I'll convert you, though,' Tony said, without looking at her. It was the first thing he had said to Angela directly, and Ruth felt a small, uncommon pang of possessiveness, almost of fear. She looked sharply at Angela who, if her face had not been so thin and anxious, might have been described as simpering. 'My father's past saving,' Tony said.

'Actually, a year or so ago I thought I'd have to chuck up the whole thing and take a job or something. Luckily, it all blew over.'

'Why?'

'Well, I mean, when it comes to being arrested at some ridiculous Socialist rally it's a bit much at his age. He's quite well known and so on. My mother was frightfully upset. I told him frankly—you don't get anywhere by throwing fireworks at the mounted police. I mean, that sort of thing's just a bore. You grow out of it at school—or you should.'

'Well,' Angela said hotly, clattering the plates on to the trolley, 'I think if a lot more people threw fireworks much more often, everyone would be much better off.'

'Nonsense,' Rex snapped. 'You don't know what you're talking about. He's perfectly right.'

'Angela's very old-fashioned,' Tony said amiably. 'It's extraordinary how many people are, even at Oxford. You find most of them have gone up straight from school, or got out of National Service in some way.' He puffed energetically at his pipe. 'One thing the Army does do for you, it makes you face facts.'

'Oh,' Angela said. 'Really!' She rushed the trolley out of the room. Rex and Tony sat opposite each other on each side of the fireplace, their legs crossed, neither of them glancing towards the door.

'I'll go and help Angela—' Ruth said. They nodded absently.

'Don't you agree with me, sir, that this doing away with National Service is a frightful mistake? I mean, frankly—'

Ruth closed the door. Angela had already begun the washing-up. Her expression was tranquil.

'You don't have to do this,' Ruth said. 'Why don't you finish your packing?'

'I've finished it. I don't mind. You dry.'

'I shan't know what—' Ruth began.

Angela, not listening, interrupted her. 'We'll go straight away if you don't mind. There's no point in hanging about.'

'No, of course not.' She dried the cups carefully.

'They get on like a house on fire, don't they?' Angela asked in a slight, strained voice.

Ruth nodded, smiling.

'Daddy obviously thinks he's wonderful.'

'Well,' Ruth asked, peering inside the teapot, 'don't you?'

'Me?' Angela stared at her, amazed. The question, so unexpected, so unlike her mother, released a hundred conflicting answers, a small chaos of emotion for which she was quite unprepared. 'Think he's wonderful?' she repeated, as though not quite sure what it meant. 'Well, I mean—I don't know—he's all right. I mean, sometimes I think so, but then other times I . . . Oh, I don't know. He's all right.'

'I see,' Ruth said. She knew far more exactly than Angela what she meant. Tony might be a stupid, infuriating bore, a bully and a prig, but this was not at the moment important. He was a man. He had always been a man, lolling in his pram at the age of one, a crack shot with an air gun at seven, an arm-twister and a hair-puller until, at the correct sort of school, he had earned the right to flog little boys who were not, in the same way, men. He would be a success. In another twenty years he might even own a house on the Common. To love him would be to hold up a heavy mirror month after month, year after year, in which he could see his own manliness reflected; to grow, behind it, older and weaker and certainly, in the end, to give way. He would

60

drive his wife mad but he would not, by this time, be all right. He would be greedy, heavy, his stupidity inexcusable, his crudeness no longer justified by a fancy haircut or an exhibition of boyish charm. He would never understand why his world thought highly of him and his wife hated him. He would never understand that he had lost his only attraction, the quality of offering pleasure, of which he was entirely ignorant. He would never understand anything, except that he ought to be loved.

'Do you like him?' Angela asked, almost timidly. 'I mean, of course you've hardly met him and you can't possibly know what he's like, but—'

Ruth put away the last plate, closed the cupboard door, took off her apron.

'You don't, do you?' Angela asked. 'I knew you wouldn't. He's exactly like Daddy. I suppose it's all very psychological or something.'

If they could have smiled then, splintered the silence with a shout of laughter, however cruel or trivial, they could have saved themselves. But Angela's long, thin face was clouded with gloom; she pushed her hands into her pockets and idled across the kitchen, standing by the window in an attitude of hopelessness and defeat, her head hanging, one foot vaguely tracing the pattern of the lino on the floor. Ruth's smile became a short, almost inaudible sigh.

'Of course I like him,' she said. 'Don't be so silly.'

There was no reply.

'In any case,' she said, 'even if I didn't, I don't see what difference it would make. After all, you're eighteen.'

Angela made a small, furious sound.

'What did you say?' Ruth asked patiently.

'Oh, I just said you're hopeless, that's all. You're

absolutely hopeless!' She ran, ungainly with trouble, out of the kitchen and pounded up the stairs. A door slammed. The cry lingered in the kitchen, vibrated in the dying sunlight, played itself out against the polished saucepans, the hard, cold surfaces. You are hopeless, hopeless.

Oh, well, Ruth thought. 'Oh, well,' she said, 'that's stale buns.' She smiled, her lips trembling. 'Stale buns. Hard cheese. Anty doughnuts.' She shrugged her shoulders, slipping off the table where she had been sitting. When she went back into the drawing-room she looked alert and well, the exhaustion of the past hour lifted. She pulled a piece of string out of her workbox, sat with her feet under her in the corner of the sofa and began playing cats' cradle with herself.

'Well, sir,' Tony said. 'It's been most interesting meeting you.' He looked sharply at Ruth. 'And you, too, Mrs. Whiting. It's the most charming house.'

'Thank you,' Ruth said, neatly turning the cradle inside out.

'I think we probably ought to go if we're going to get there before dark. I suppose Angela's getting ready or something?'

Ruth smiled at him radiantly. 'I expect so.'

'Oh, for God's sake,' Rex muttered. He levered himself out of his chair and went to the door. 'Angela!' he roared. 'Hurry up, can't you? Tony's waiting!'

'Do you remember,' Ruth asked gently, 'how to make a Double King's Crown?'

'What's that?' Tony asked suspiciously.

'I know it comes after Fish in a Dish, but—'

'Angela!' Rex roared.

'Oh, yes. I know. It's like this. You see?' She held up

the complex pattern of string for the boy's approval. Their eyes met, a moment of full knowledge, of deep hostility. 'It's awfully easy,' Ruth said. 'A child can do it. In fact, they often do.'

'Really?' Tony said. 'Most interesting.'

Angela came slowly downstairs, carrying a small canvas grip. She had put on her duffle-coat, but had not bothered to brush her hair or wash the dried tears off her face.

'Come on, then,' she said. 'Let's go, for heaven's sake.'

'You look terrible,' Rex said. 'Why can't you tidy yourself up a bit?' He turned to Ruth, who crumpled the string in her hand and stood up. 'Why can't you make her do something about herself? She looks terrible.'

Angela shrugged her shoulders. Tony wound himself hastily inside his scarf.

'Well,' he said, 'thanks very much for the tea.'

Ruth hardly noticed him. She said, across the distance of the hall, 'Good-bye, darling.'

'Good-bye.' Angela turned, hesitated. She felt relief and regret, a moment's unhappiness. They hurried towards each other, their embrace an awkward scuffle watched with embarrassment by the two men. 'Don't worry,' Angela said awkwardly.

'Of course not. Take care of yourself.'

'All right for money?' Rex asked, making a vague gesture towards his wallet.

'Yes, thank you. Oh, lord, here come people. Let's go.'

Ruth stepped back from the door and watched them climb on to the Vespa. Then, silently on soft shoes, she ran upstairs. She closed her bedroom door and hurried to the window in time to see them swerving away between the hedges, the Johnsons standing and waving after them. She listened for a moment and then heard voices, Betty's exorbitant laugh, as they walked across the hall. The sitting-room door shut. It was time for another drink, another saucer of potato crisps. The church bells chimed distantly in the hazy air, rooms were adrift with dead newspapers, the German girls were out. A great yawn swallowed the Common, sucking it into winter, stripping its trees, blasting its lush gardens.

You are hopeless. Hopeless. A nightmare was beginning, far away in the house, in the empty rooms. Silence was accumulating. She could feel it waiting, growing deeper, more deadly. The room was full of dangers, her own reflection in the mirror, her own voice, her own hand stretching out in front of her. She picked up the musical box, holding it carefully. She turned the handle and heard the tune dropping note by note, water into an empty well. She carried it over to the dressing-table and sat down, turning the handle round and round. In a little while her lips moved soundlessly, forming words remote and innocent as the melody itself . . .

> . . . Baby Bunting
> Daddy's gone a-hunting,
> Gone to fetch a rabbit skin
> To wrap his Baby Bunting in,
> Bye Baby Bunting—

She played it over and over, terrified of stopping and hearing, again, silence.

Chapter 11

THE FIRST STAGE of the nightmare is losing the ability to believe in insignificance. Consciousness is sharpened to a point in which nothing is trivial but every moment, every detail, has the same unbearable quality of dread. In this condition of despair there are no crises. The merciful censor of memory has broken down and everything is recalled with equal horror, the broken nail becomes a jagged pointer to the senselessness of living, the most commonplace remark releases, without warning, the grief or terror of a lifetime. But still the days pile up, one on top of the other, in an orderly fashion; the weeks are marked by a red Sunday and the months have names. It is necessary to eat and sleep. It is necessary to prepare for the future, even if this is only done by drawing in breath so that it may, in a moment, be exhaled and breathed again. The moral judgement delivered on this state of unhappiness is as severe as that pronounced on the lunatics of Bedlam. Lost, it says with smug disgust, all sense of proportion. Which is exactly true.

Ruth was alone now, without the children, without Angela, without Rex. Nobody judged her; nobody answered when she spoke. She watched, flattened beside the landing window, women waiting on the front doorstep, women who had thought of dropping in—and the moment they had gone, walking briskly off through the gate with their dogs winding leads round their ankles, she longed to see them, often called out, knowing it was too late. When the telephone rang she was paralysed, standing and watching it until the last ring sounded and only then moving her hand tentatively towards the receiver.

She never stopped feeling afraid. Sometimes the fear pulled tighter, as though she had tried to wrench away; sometimes it was deceptively slack, the knot of anxiety bearable until she tried to move backwards or forwards, into the past or the future. She thought of going up to London, telephoning Rex, asking for help. *Rex, listen, I'm not well.* There was silence. *Rex, I thought I should tell you . . . Well? Well? What is it?*

'*Rex, listen. I think I'm going to have a baby.*'

'*What the hell am I supposed to do about it?*'

'*If you aren't prepared to do the decent thing, Whiting, I'll wreck your career, by God, I'll wreck your career.*'

'*But naturally, sir, there's no alternative. I must say, sir, that I resent your implication—*'

And her mother, who believed in God: '*It is always darkest before dawn and as it is the baby will be far too premature, I think perhaps a simple print dress under the circumstances and I always hoped for a pretty white wedding. Ingratitude, dearest, is very hard to bear but it's lucky your poor father is due for retirement and County Wicklow, I'm told, is full of very nice people, of course you won't be able to come over there with a young baby but it's an ill wind that has no silver lining, providing you pray for forgiveness.*'

She whimpered, holding her head between her wrists.

'*You're a fool, Ruth, that's your trouble. Why can't you stop that brat crying? What's it crying for, anyway? What?*'

'*I don't know . . .*'

'*Don't you love me any more? Eh, Ruthie? Don't you love me?*'

'*I don't know—*'

'*What d'you think I married you for, anyway? Because you were so damned attractive? What? I married you because you were in pod, and you know it. You didn't have any objection then, did you? Well, did you?*'

'*I don't know . . . I don't know—*'

And then a floorboard would creak upstairs; a dog bark in the distance; a scrap of paper writhe, dying, in the fireplace. She would watch it, weeping, intolerably bereaved. A scrap of paper. Nothing.

Jane trapped her in the afternoon. In the afternoon, the only wife at this end of the Common with a small child, Jane went for walks, for torturous creeps, stone by stone and stick by stick up the lane and back again. They shuffled through the gate at half-past three and explored the lawn for some time before approaching the french window leading into the Whitings' drawing-room. The house, except for its thin signal of smoke, looked dead. Jane peered through the window and saw Ruth crouched at the end of the sofa, the upper half of her body hanging over the sofa arm.

'Ruth's asleep,' she muttered, trying to pull the child away.

Baby banged with the flat of her hand on the window.

'Come back tomorrow,' Jane pleaded.

Baby kicked the window with the stubby toe of her

walking shoe. In one movement, swift as guilt, Ruth was on her feet. Her mouth opened soundlessly, she stepped forward, pushed at her hair, looking back towards the door. Jane smiled faintly, made exaggerated gestures of regret. As Ruth came to the window, slowly emerging out of the shadowed room, Jane was horrified to see that she was still in her dressing-gown. Still? Perhaps she put it on to rest in. The bolts were drawn, the window opened.

'. . . So dreadfully sorry, love, it's all her fault. Were you asleep?'

'Yes,' Ruth said. She laughed quickly, pushing at her hair again. 'Yes, I must have been, how stupid of me, what's the time?'

'I don't know,' Jane said, uneasily snatching at the child's struggling arm. 'I mean, about half-past three I should think. I'm so terribly sorry to—oh, lord, I am sorry.' Baby had wrenched free and squirmed in through the window, climbed on an armchair, sat with her gaitered legs stiff like a visiting bishop.

'Tea?' she asked coldly, looking round, seeing no sign of it.

'No, no,' Jane said hopelessly, 'we haven't come for tea.'

'But of course—' Ruth began. 'There might be some biscuits—'

When she came back, with tea made and a saucer of broken chocolate biscuits she had found in the bottom of a tin, Baby was still waiting.

'I'm so sorry,' Ruth said. 'There isn't anything—I don't usually—and not even any milk.' Her voice was at the breaking point of despair. She put the tray down, not looking at either of them. 'I'm so dreadfully sorry.'

'Oh, good heavens, that's all right.'

'Where's the sandwiches?' Baby enquired, peering round the tray.

'Oh, God—' Jane moaned.

'There aren't any,' Ruth said. This statement of fact reduced the child to shocked silence. She sat with the saucer of biscuits balanced on her outstretched legs, staring at Ruth and not moving, for at least three minutes. Then, piece by piece, she began to eat the biscuits, planning revenge.

'How's it been?' Jane asked quickly, knowing time was short. 'We haven't seen you for days. Angela's gone, I imagine?'

'Yes. Yes, she went on Sunday.'

'You don't look well, you know. You look ghastly. Is anything the matter?'

Tears raged behind her eyes. 'No,' she said, 'I don't know, I mean no, nothing.' A tremendous effort, the bright, trembling voice of someone taking tea on a tightrope. 'How's Richard? I haven't seen you since—'

'Oh, that ghastly weekend with Herb and Maxine. Could you *believe* Maxine? What a frightening girl. She thought you were absolutely wonderful.'

'Did she?' A quick, unbelieving laugh. 'I thought it was Rex—'

'Oh, you don't want to take any notice of that. It's just a nervous tic, she can't help it.' She looked sharply at Ruth. No, nobody could be such a fool. That podgy child upset her? She'd upset Betty Johnson all right, but nobody in their right mind— 'And how's Angela? Still rushing about on that Vespa?'

'Yes. Yes, I expect so.'

The telephone began to ring out in the hall. Jane and

Baby both became alert, pleased and bright as though hearing a familiar voice.

'It's the telephone,' Jane said.

'Yes.'

It rang on, happily crowing an invitation, a scandal, a piece of important news. Why did she sit there, looking helplessly about? What was the matter with her? 'Aren't you going to answer it?'

'Yes. Yes, I suppose so.'

She got up slowly. Jane stared at her. She went slowly out into the hall, but the telephone kept ringing. At last, when the suspense had become almost unbearable, it stopped.

She picked up the receiver, but said nothing. The voice at the other end rapped, 'Hullo? Hullo? Are you there? What the hell's the matter with this damned line?'

She sat down, holding the receiver with both hands.

'Hullo?' he shouted.

She ran her tongue over her drp lips. 'Rex?'

'What the hell's the matter with the 'phone? I've tried to ring you about six times. Are you out all day, or what?'

She shook her head.

'What? Are you there?'

'Yes.'

'I said I've tried to ring you six times.'

'I'm sorry.'

'The line's terrible, I can't hear you. Can you hear me?'

'Yes. Yes, I can hear you.'

'Well, listen, I shan't be coming down this weekend. I've got a couple of consultations tomorrow and I'm playing golf with Craxton on Sunday. Is that all right?'

She nodded helplessly.

'I said is that all right? Did you hear me?'

'Yes.'

'Good. Then I'll see you next week. Everything all right?'

'Rex, listen—'

'You'd better get on to the engineers. I tried to ring you six times. Will you do that?'

'But I—'

'Good God, it's not hard. Just ring the operator.'

'Rex, listen—'

He had rung off. She stared stupidly at the receiver. Her mouth twitched uncertainly, as though she might smile.

'Ruth? Can I take her to—? Ruth. Are you all right?'

She nodded, twisting her hands round the receiver. Her whole body was shaking, crushed together on the small chair.

'Ruth! Ruth, what's the matter?'

She looked up, her eyes dilated with the pitiful alarm of someone falling. 'I—'

'Come, now, come along, I'll take you upstairs. Come, now, it's all right, don't cry—' The little square woman supported her, bearing her slight weight, edging her towards the stairs. Baby, abandoned, began screaming. For the first time in her life, Jane hated her. 'Oh, shut up!' she hissed. 'Shut up for once, can't you?'

OOD MORNING,' Miss de Beer said, just loudly enough to wake Ruth up. She pulled back the curtains in front of a wall of fog. 'Not a very nice morning, I'm afraid.' She switched on the fire and the bedside lamp. Ruth saw her sallow, mournful face with the sunken eyes swimming, disembodied, above the abrupt halo of light. 'Breakfast and four nice letters,' she said, with her trim, vicarage enunciation. 'And the doctor is here already, I asked him to wait.'

'What's the time?' Ruth struggled up out of the warm covers, the long, drugged sleep.

'Half-past ten. We'll tidy you in a jiffy. I brought a cup for the doctor, you see.'

'Yes. Thank you.'

'And the egg has had a good four minutes.'

'Thank you.'

'Feeling all right this morning? Quite chirpy?'

How do I know? Chirpy? She pulled the tray, with its grubby cloth, its naked boiled egg and sticky jar of marmalade, on to her knees. Miss de Beer was her wardress, engaged by Rex to look after her. How long had she been here? Weeks? Months? She had seen a few leaves on the trees yesterday. Was it November?

'I told him you were just a wee bit weepy last night,' Miss de Beer said cautiously.

Ruth picked up the letters and put them down again. 'Yes,' she said. 'Well, ask him to come up, would you?'

John Phillips was a portly, bald man, bored to death with medicine. He liked hunting, cricket and, rather curiously, folk dancing. Jigging about with bells tied round his stout legs he sweated with a kind of forlorn, country gaiety. His treatment of Ruth over the past four weeks had been simple: pull your socks up, think of those fine kids of yours, hope for the best. He had prescribed various brightly-coloured pills and, after leafing through a handbook on psychology, suggested ordering a loom. At really tricky moments—and there had been some, indeed—he had brought in God as a kind of senior consultant. His faith in God was ornate and sentimental, like a woman's. He was popular on the Common where he was suspected, among the wives, of some obscure but interesting sexual peculiarity.

'Morning, Ruth.' He brought with him, he hoped, the raw, livid feeling of fog, of difficulties and responsibilities and having to be somewhere on time. 'I thought you'd be up and packing by now. How d'you feel?'

'All right.' He had tried so hard; she didn't want to let him down. She added a smile. 'Much better, really.'

'Beer says you had a bit of a weep last night. What was that for?'

'Oh . . . Nothing. I don't remember. Really, nothing.'

'Well,' he clapped and rubbed his hands together, 'this trip to Antibes will cure all that. You'll be a new woman when you come back, I promise you.'

'Yes, John.' A trip to Antibes—did he really believe in it?

'It'll all seem different, you know.'

The Common? The house? A house where the walls, built for protection, had become barriers surrounding pits of solitude? What would be different about it? How could it possibly change?

'Yes, John. I'm sure it will.'

'And you've got to think of those kids, you know. Angela, Julian, Mike. They want you to get better. They're worth making an effort for, aren't they?'

She nodded emphatically. You're so lucky to have children; for sixteen weeks in every year to have children. Here they come, unfamiliar, large, extraordinary, breaking in on a fragile state of anxiety; and there they go, leaving the pieces, leaving the door open for an inrush of silence. 'Of course,' she said. 'Of course.'

'And then,' he said heartily, 'you'll be getting ready for Christmas. Plenty to think about, plenty to plan for.'

Thinking. Planning. Preparing. Twelve times every year your body becomes elaborately prepared, for nothing. Living is a perpetual preparation for nothing. Stick flags in the bridge rolls, check the store cupboard, empty the ash-trays; have everything in order, have a manicure, send little messages over short distances by telephone. When you move there is a rustle of old shopping lists, like dead leaves; when you sit still there is the terror of time slipping away. You must get on. You run about inside the high walls. You prepare to prepare to prepare—

'Oh, you'll make a success of it, I'm certain of that. You've done very well already. No reason why you shouldn't give yourself a pat on the back from time to time, you know.'

So you look back to congratulate yourself. But there's nothing there. It is all the same as it was before. You have been busy with handfuls of air, moving shadows, disciplining emptiness.

'You're still a young woman. You've got a good sense of humour, a pretty face, a fine family. What more do you want?'

'Nothing, John. Nothing.'

'As I've told you before, I'm no trick-cyclist and I don't think that's what you need. If I did, I'd have sent you off to one long ago.'

'Yes, I know.'

'Well—' He didn't feel he had really succeeded. 'If there's ever anything I can do,' he said, 'you know you only have to ask.'

'Thank you. You've been wonderful, John.' She looked at her hands lying on the blanket. 'I'm sorry I've been such a nuisance.'

'Nonsense. You haven't been a nuisance at all. One thing about this ghastly job of mine, you can occasionally get someone out of a tight corner. Makes the whole thing worth while, you know. I'd sooner give a touch of sympathy and understanding than all the pills in Christendom.' He looked at his watch, reluctant to get on with his round, peering down screaming children's throats, sounding their flaccid chests, checking the progress of dull pregnancies. 'Well, I can't stay here gossiping and you've got your packing to do. What time do you leave tomorrow?'

'About eight, I think. Rex is coming down this evening.'

'I'll drop in before dinner and have a word with him. I don't want you worried while you're away. Any problems that may crop up with the kids and so on—well, Rex must deal with them.'

'Yes, John.'

'Just try to think of this little affair of yours as though it's a sprained ankle. Rest it up, and it'll get better. We don't want any complications, you know. I'll drop in this evening.'

'All right.'

He picked up the musical box and turned the handle a few times. 'Pretty thing. Where did it come from?'

'I don't remember,' she said, in a kind of agony of patience.

'Well. See you this evening, then.'

'Yes, John. Thank you. Good-bye.'

When he had gone she slumped back on the pillows. Now, at last, she could sleep again. Sleep and sleep and forget everything. She shut her eyes, driving herself back into sleep.

'Oh dear, oh dear, you've spilled your coffee. You haven't eaten your egg. You haven't looked at your nice letters. Oh, Mrs. Whiting!'

'I want to go to sleep.'

'No, no, we can't have that, now. Lots to be done, lots of happy things to look forward to. Come along, now. Up we sit, two little pills. That's better—' She looked critically at her arrangement of Ruth, propped upright and angry. 'Nothing's hard if you try and we've had quite enough sleep for the time being.'

'But I'm tired.'

'No, no, you're not tired at all,' Miss de Beer laughed indulgently. 'Just a little bit muzzy with the sleeping tablets, I expect. I'll turn on your bath and you read your letters and in five minutes you'll feel as right as rain.' She pushed the letters into Ruth's hand and stood over her. 'Now there you are. A nice invitation, you see. Something to look forward to.'

A white card, with neat gold lettering. *Ralph Rackworth requests the pleasure of Mr. and Mrs. Rex Whiting's company at a Rock and Roll party to be held at Rackworth House on Saturday, November 30th at 9.30 p.m. No decorations. No swords.*

'I say,' Miss de Beer said, peering. 'What fun!'

'Perhaps you'd like to go,' Ruth suggested. 'I shan't be here, anyway.'

Offended, Miss de Beer marched off to the bathroom. The next letter was on thick pink paper, the words drawn, rather than written, in violet ink.

> *Dear Mrs. Whiting,*
>
> *I am so awfully sorry to hear that you have been ill and I thought I would write a little note—I do hope you are better now—The weather is so dreadful that it must be nice to be in bed although I expect you are longing to be up again—Well, this is really just to say how sorry I am to hear you have been ill as I did so enjoy meeting you and coming to your lovely house— With kind regards and best wishes for your recovery.*
> >   *Yours very sincerely,*
> >   *Maxine O'Donovan.*

She opened the next one reluctantly. Letters from the children, photographs of them, almost the mention of them could start the pain again, the shameful weeping. Sickeningly, as she read, the words became blurred, the sheet of lined paper trembled.

> *Dear Mum,*
>
> *I hope you are better now. It's a pity you couldn't come down. Mike went out with the Robinsons last*

weekend and stuffed himself as usual. I didn't go out. I hope you are feeling better. The weather has been awful and about thirty people are in the San with flu but I haven't had it yet. Could you send some Polos and Refreshers and two bags of sherbert and some more stamps. I would like some boxing gloves for Christmas if that's all right. Mike is too busy (!) to write but he says he will next week. I hope you are feeling quite chirpy again.

Lots of Love,
Julian.

Someone else must see about getting the sweets. Someone else must go to the post office. Someone else must write to him, buy boxing gloves . . . She turned her face into the pillow, hating herself so passionately that her weakness, her inability to punish herself, was unendurable.

'Your bath, Mrs. Whiting.'

'Go away!'

'What's the matter?' She picked up Julian's letter from the floor, scanned through it quickly. 'Just a nice letter from your little boy, nothing to worry about.'

'Go away!'

'And this one,' Miss de Beer almost shouted, 'from your daughter, I should think. It's an Oxford postmark. It says Urgent.'

Ruth lay still. Urgent? Angela?

'Shall I read it to you?' Miss de Beer had torn open the envelope.

'No.' She sat up, snatched the piece of paper. It was torn out of an exercise book. She held it, unopened, watching Miss de Beer walk across the room to the window, unnecessarily fuss the curtains. Then, almost furtively, she unfolded it.

Darling Mummy,

This is terribly important. I must see you. I'll be home on Friday evening, about six. I'll explain why I can't 'phone. It is really *important and please I must see you* alone. *Sorry for the rush.*

All love,

A.

I hope your flu or whatever it was is better. Can you make up some story for Daddy—I must see you alone.

'Well,' Miss de Beer said, 'the fog is clearing. That's a good omen. Your bath will be getting cold, I'm afraid.'

'Is it Friday?' Ruth asked, in a curiously flat voice.

'That's right,' Miss de Beer said, brightly congratulating her.

'My—my daughter's coming home for the night.'

'Tonight?'

'Yes.'

'To say good-bye, I suppose. Now isn't that exciting. You see, there's always something to look forward to, isn't there?'

Ruth got slowly out of bed. She looked vaguely round the room, as though only just noticing where she was. 'Perhaps you would make a hot-water bottle—her bed will need airing.'

'Of course, just leave it all to me. Your dressing-gown is on the bed, Mrs. Whiting.'

'I shall have to get her room ready.'

'Now don't worry. There's nothing to worry about. Your slippers, Mrs. Whiting—'

'And while she is here please don't talk about—I mean, discuss me with her.'

'Naturally, Mrs. Whiting, I wouldn't dream—'

'And Miss de Beer. When you ring up Turners for the order would you ask them to send four packets of Polos, four packets of Refreshers and six bags of—'

'Sherbet?'

'Yes. Sherbet.'

'Your daughter's been a tonic to you,' Miss de Beer cried cheerfully. 'Just what the doctor ordered. You look better already, I'm sure of it.'

'There's just one more thing.' Her voice was steady but her legs were shaking.

'Yes, Mrs. Whiting?'

The shout, the yell of anger was audible under the carefully flat tones. 'Will you leave me alone, for God's sake? Will you leave me alone?'

'But the packing—'

'The packing can wait. It isn't important.'

The door slammed. Ruth's hand flew to her mouth; over her cupped hand her eyes shone, awed by this small, uncertainly executed act of courage.

Chapter 13

As ANGELA WALKED round the house to the back door she could hear the Vespa tearing away through the darkness. Oh lord, she thought, they'll hear that for sure. She was cold all the way through; her mouth was numb and her eyes felt like two pebbles, petrified by cold; when she moved her jaw her cheeks felt as though they were cracking like cat's ice. She opened the back door, fell over the gum boots. Why, she thought for the hundredth time, they can't have a light by the back door . . . There was an unusual smell, rubber and wet cabbage, the smell of school corridors. She went into the kitchen, blinking at the bright light, expecting to see her mother. Instead, in a print apron, beating something in a bowl, a stranger. They were both shocked.

'Oh,' Angela said. She sensed, without actually noticing, mess, grease, unwashed milk bottles. 'Where's Mrs. Whiting?'

'I suppose you must be—?'

'I'm Angela. Where's Mrs. Whiting?'

'I think she's in the drawing-room. I—'

'Has my father arrived yet?'

'No, no, I don't think so.'

'But he is coming this evening?'

'Oh, yes, because your mother is—'

The rest of the house, anyway, seemed just as it always was. She left the green baize door swinging and walked quickly along the passage. The telephone was on the table, the clothesbrushes hung each side of the mirror, the hunting scenes were still symmetrically placed on the wall, the brass knob of the drawing-room door was still dented and polished. Extraordinary that all this should exist when she wasn't there; that whatever was happening to her they went on dusting and polishing and straightening the pictures as though it mattered. She hesitated for a moment, but there was no alternative. She opened the door. Her mother turned, jumped up from the sofa. Oh God, don't let her make a fuss.

'Darling—' Their faces met briefly. 'How cold you are. I didn't hear you come. How did you get from the station? Did you get a taxi? I thought perhaps in this fog they wouldn't come up here, but since I didn't know what time—'

'There isn't any fog now. Tony brought me.' She's at her worst, why can't one ever come home without it seeming like a bloody miracle? She knelt in front of the fire, clasping her arms across her chest. Now that she was here, actually about to tell this thing, she felt lightheaded, unable to take it at all seriously. The anxiety, the despair of the past week had changed, the moment she entered this room, into a great yawn.

'By the way, who's that peculiar woman in the kitchen?'

'Oh, she's a sort of a—housekeeper. She came to look after things while I was ill. Where is Tony?'

'He's gone.' She yawned, shivered, rubbed her arms. 'Do you think I could have a drink or something?'

82

'Of course.' Her mother jumped up again. She looks terrible, Angela thought resentfully. Old. She hasn't looked at me once. 'What would you like?'

'Oh—gin, sherry, anything there is.'

'Well'—the familiar, nervous laugh—'which?'

'Anything. I don't mind. What's her name, anyway?'

'Miss de Beer.'

'Why *de* Beer?'

'I don't know.'

No, of course you wouldn't. 'How ridiculous.'

She shivered, sipping her drink like medicine. Her mother was back on the sofa now, sitting bolt upright, her hands in her lap, waiting. If only she would ask. Any normal mother, surely, would come right out with it: 'Well, why have you come home?' 'Well, really, it's a terribly corny situation but—' Digging her finger into the thick pile of the hearthrug, hiding her face with the heavy, lank hair, Angela also waited. It was a battle of silence.

'Did you—' her mother began at last. Angela looked up quickly, swept with relief. Her mother's face was grey, glistening, the pale mouth struggling to form words. 'Is anything the matter, you said—'

'Yes, I know.' How did one put it? What were the right, the least melodramatic words? It wasn't easy at all. It was horrible. There was no way out. She rushed at it. 'I'm going to have a baby. That's all.'

Silence.

'I'm pregnant,' she insisted; and then, with a terrible lurch of fear, 'Do you understand?'

Her mother got up and walked across the room, moving carefully round the sofa and table until she got to the distant, shadowed corner. 'Yes,' she said. She seemed to pause, considering something. 'Would you like another drink?'

'No, thank you. Unless you've got some tomato juice.'

'There's some in the fridge. I can easily get it.'

'No. Really. It doesn't matter.'

Neither of them said anything for a full minute. *Why* doesn't she say something? Yell at me. Show how shocked she is? Punish me in some way? A bitter sense of injustice, worse for being unreasonable, made her want to drum her fists on the floor, howl, scream, do anything to break the silence.

'Are you quite sure?'

'A friend of Tony's examined me. He's a medical student. He was quite sure.'

'He might be wrong.'

'He's not wrong! He's certain!'

'How—how long did he say?'

'Two months. I know that anyway.'

'Why?'

'Because it was that night we went to the fair. The day the kids went back to school. After that I was, you know, careful.'

She was trying her best. As Tony kept saying, there was no point in losing your head. Tony? It was easy for him. Easy.

'Why were you so stupid?'

'What?' She wrenched her head up, stared incredulously across the room.

'Why were you such a *fool?*'

Her mother was trembling. She could see her trembling. The ineffectual, vague, silly little woman with her neat chintz life, her safe, smug little life, her balmy games and her nerves and her idiotic laugh was angry. It was incredible. She forgot that she had wanted her to be angry. She only knew that again, again, she was being rejected, abandoned, betrayed by someone who ought to love her. There were no words for it. She knew that what she was shouting was futile, that she looked ugly and clumsy and wasn't doing any good. It didn't matter.

'. . . That's all you can say, isn't it! I come all this way to tell you because I think you might help and all you can do is shout at me. You don't think about *me*, do you? You don't care what *I'm* feeling. You never had to face anything like this in the whole of your life, it's something that doesn't happen to people like us, isn't it? What will the Tanners think, and the Johnsons and the bloody Wilmington-Smiths —oh, my *God*, I should have known!'

'Stop it!'

They stared at each other for a moment. A coal slid down in the fire and footsteps approached along the passage. Miss de Beer's head appeared round the door simultaneously with her cheery knock.

'We've met before,' she said, nodding brightly at Angela. 'Time you were in bed, Mrs. Whiting. You know I promised the doctor.'

'Oh, go away!'

'I beg your pardon?'

'I shan't go to bed till after dinner tonight. I'm perfectly all right. I'll tell Doctor Phillips when he comes—'

'That's hardly the point, Mrs. Whiting. I'm responsible for you, and with that long journey tomorrow I absolutely insist that you go to bed. Your mother has not been at all well,' she snapped at Angela. 'It is quite essential that she doesn't overtire herself. She has to be up very early in the morning.'

'Why? What journey?' She turned, appalled, to her mother. 'You're not going away, are you?'

'Your mother is going to the south of France tomorrow,' Miss de Beer said smugly, as though it were a punishment Ruth richly deserved. 'For a rest. The journey will be very tiring.'

'But you can't! When are you coming back? Nobody told me!'

They were all looking from one to the other. Loose ends, blind alleys, feelings torn out and left naked in the air.

The front door slammed.

'Anybody home?' Rex bellowed cheerfully.

For a second, none of them moved. Then Miss de Beer, head down, scuttled away. Ruth stepped out into the passage.

'Yes,' she said. 'Angela's here too.'

'Angela? What on earth is *she* doing?' Then, seeing them standing there, seeming to look at him with trust, he made a supreme effort: 'Well, old thing, how nice to see you,' and kissed them both.

Chapter 14

AVE YOU HEARD the news?' He siphoned soda into his whisky, came round to the fire and stood beaming down on them. 'Your mother's off to the south of France tomorrow. How about that?'

'I know,' Angela said. She lunged towards the door. 'I'll go and wash. I'm absolutely filthy. What do I say to that frightful woman if I see her?'

'What frightful woman?' Rex asked.

'Just smile,' Ruth said. 'You don't need to say anything.'

'What frightful woman?'

'Miss de Beer.'

'What's frightful about her?'

'Nothing.'

'Oh, well—' He finished his drink, thinking how soon all this would be over. 'We've got to be at the airport at ten. That means leaving here around half-past seven. You're packed and everything, I suppose?'

How am I going to do this? Carefully, carefully. She plaited her fingers together. She bowed her head.

'You seem very anxious to get rid of me.'

'Oh, come now, Ruthie—'

'I wasn't so well this week. Miss de Beer's bound to tell you.'

'I'm sorry to hear that. This trip's going to put you right, though.'

'I'm frightened. I'm awfully frightened of going.'

'No, no, you're not. You just think you are.'

He smiled indulgently, lighting a cigar.

Ruth glanced at him cautiously. His heavy, still-handsome face was relaxed. She could understand why he was a success, why so many actresses, debutantes, mothers of debutantes, fashion models and child stars opened their precious mouths to him. He had sympathy for them; he charmed them with gentleness and skill. If he was able to drill a tooth without pain, he must be able to understand suffering. Wasn't that true?

Of course not. She knew it wasn't true. Nevertheless she moved, taking Angela's place on the floor, smiling up at him.

'How are the Craxtons?'

'Oh, fine. I went down there one night, had an excellent meal. They sent their love and so on.'

'I had a letter from that girl this morning. The one who was staying with the Tanners.'

His face hardened. 'What girl?'

'You know, the blonde, the one with the funny voice.'

He put down his glass, lit his cigar again.

'What on earth was she writing to you for?'

'I don't know. Somebody must have told her I was ill. I thought it was rather sweet of her.'

'Was that all?'

'What do you mean?'

'Was that all she said?'

'Yes.'

He got up, took his glass for another drink.

'Why the hell can't we have dinner? What's that woman up to? Can't she ever have it ready on time?'

'It's only half-past seven. We don't usually have it till eight.'

He stayed fussing on the other side of the room. She got up from the floor.

'I'm not going tomorrow,' she said wearily. There was, after all, no other way to say it.

'What?'

'I'm not going tomorrow. I'm not going to Antibes.'

He stared at her, then laughed. 'Of course you're going, my dear. Don't be absurd.'

'I'm not. I'm sorry.'

'Now Ruth. Don't start imagining things again. You're going to get on that 'plane and sit in the sun and fill yourself up with food—I envy you. I must admit. I envy you.'

She moved two Staffordshire spaniels slightly to the centre of the mantelpiece.

'But I'm not going.'

There was a moment's silence. He was trying to control himself. The pause was a genuine effort.

'Might I ask why?'

'Of course.' She turned. He was grasping the back of the sofa, his face slowly flushing. 'I want to stay here.'

'And why do you want to stay here?'

'Because I do. That's all, because I do.'

'My God!' he sighed desperately. Ten slow seconds went by. 'Look, Ruth. You've had a nervous collapse. You aren't capable of taking decisions like this. I don't think you quite realise—'

'But you are willing to send me off, alone, to Antibes?'

'You agreed to it, didn't you?'

'But I'm not capable of taking decisions. You just said so.'

'Christ Almighty, why don't you want to go? Who needs you here? What difference does it make?'

She said nothing.

'You've got a reason, haven't you? You're not so dotty as you make out. You've got a reason.'

She said nothing.

'All right. Out with it, then. Come out with it, woman.'

I shall have to. What else can I say? She stared at him, not knowing what to do.

'Who have you been talking to?'

'Talking to?'

'Oh, stop being so bloody innocent.'

She knew, suddenly, that he had forgotten Angela's existence. He was so locked, barred, bolted in himself that you could die in front of him and he wouldn't believe it.

'I don't know what you're talking about,' she said blankly. She allowed her voice to tremble, her hands to fly together in despair. 'I just don't want to go to Antibes. I don't want to go. I don't want to.'

'The doctor is here,' Miss de Beer said, opening the door but not coming into the room.

'Well, bring him in,' Rex groaned. 'Why don't you bring him in?'

John Phillips came hurrying towards Ruth, his bald head glinting. As he came, with hands outstretched to comfort and order her, his face kind and distressed, she felt a tremendous relief, the lifting of a burden so heavy that, released from it, she almost staggered and fell into his arms.

'Oh, John.'

'What's the matter? What's wrong?'

90

'She has decided,' Rex said, 'not to go to Antibes to-morrow.'

'He won't believe me,' she wailed, knowing she was acting it badly, with faint tones of an amateur. 'He won't believe me. I feel so ill, John. I feel so frightened.'

'We'd better get you upstairs. Come on.'

All the way up the stairs she leant heavily on his arm. He opened the bedroom door, switched on the light. She closed the door smartly. He jumped, alarmed, feeling himself trapped.

'I'm sorry,' she said in a flat voice. 'I'm all right, but I had to talk to you. It's not me. It's Angela.'

IT WASN'T until his car snorted away down the drive that she moved, lifting her head out of her hands. Disgust was a stale taste in her mouth.

'You would really advise her to do this thing? Your own daughter? Good God, Ruth, I'm sorry. You make me sick.'

It hadn't even been worth trying. She might have known. She got up and dragged herself across the room to the bathroom, washed her face and hands, walked slowly down the corridor towards Angela's room.

'Hullo.' Angela looked up from the floor, littered with magazines. 'I was just looking at these.' Guilty, as though she shouldn't have been.

'Oh. Yes. People brought them when I was—when I was in bed.'

'What was the matter with you, anyway? All this mystery.'

'There's no mystery.' She sat down on the bed. Healthy girls in hand-knitted jumpers grinned up at her. What to tell your daughter. How to deal with those difficult times. If you have a worrying personal problem and need advice . . . 'It wasn't anything. I'm all right now.'

'Are you really going to France tomorrow?'

'No. No, I'm not going.'

'I'm sorry—I mean if it's because of me—'

'I didn't want to go anyway.'

'Oh, good. That's all right then.'

'Look, Angela. The doctor was just here. You know, John Phillips.'

'Yes?'

'I—I did a terribly stupid thing. I mean, I told him about you.'

'Oh.' A slight hesitation. 'Well, that was probably sensible. Why do you think it was stupid?'

'Because—' She got up, moved where she couldn't be seen. 'If this is true—I mean, what are you going to do about it? Do you want to marry Tony?'

'No, of course not.'

'Why?'

'Because I can't stand him any more. Good heavens, you don't really think I should, do you?'

'No,' Ruth said.

'Well, that's something, anyway.'

'But other people might.'

'I don't give a damn about other people.' Her voice became suddenly shrill. 'My God, you haven't told Daddy, have you?'

'No.'

'Because he'd have me married in two minutes. You know he would. I couldn't possibly explain. You promise you haven't?'

'Yes, of course.'

'I couldn't bear it, you know. I'd sooner die. I'd sooner leave Oxford and have the baby. Honestly I would.'

'Yes, but—'

'I just hate him at the moment. I despise him. I wouldn't marry him if he was the last man on earth.'

'All right,' Ruth said. 'I realise that.'

Angela looked up. Slowly, a disruption of her whole face, she grinned. 'Oh. Oh, I see what you mean.'

'About what?'

'You asked old Phillips to help us fix it. He wouldn't. He was shocked. Is that it?'

'Yes,' Ruth said wretchedly. 'That's more or less it. I'm sorry—'

'But why? I mean, why wouldn't he?'

'Well, it's against the law for one thing—'

'Oh, nonsense. Nobody really believes that. I mean, if you need to have an abortion you're going to have it whether it's against the law or not, aren't you? Like—' she made a vague gesture—'like cheating the income tax or something.'

'So you do—that is what you want to do?'

'Well, of course!' Bewildered, like someone asked whether they wanted to go on living. 'I mean—what else can I do?'

'I—' I don't know, she was going to say. She didn't say it. She bent and began picking up the magazines. 'What about Tony? What does he think?' As though it mattered. She put the magazines neatly on top of each other, levelling their edges.

'He doesn't think anything. He said I should ask you. I'm meeting him in Ramsbridge tomorrow morning. If you've got any ideas, he says, we should have a conference about money.'

'About money?'

'Well. It's expensive, isn't it? There's an old woman in

94

Cowley charges fifty pounds and that's just with a catheter or something.'

Why didn't you go to her, then? Why didn't you work it out for yourself; go away, as girls in trouble are supposed to do; be secretive, lie to me; be responsible for destroying your child, since you were responsible and grown-up enough to conceive it?

'You're not to go to any old woman in Cowley,' she said. 'You're not to. Do you understand?'

'Is there a better way then?'

The longing to give in, to sit down and cry that she didn't know, was like a dreadful desire for sleep. She had to keep standing, walking, doing something.

'You could have it adopted,' she said, distraught, as though she were talking about something else, as though she had changed the subject and was now suggesting a different-coloured wallpaper, an alteration in the room.

'You don't really mean that?'

'No.'

'Is that what Phillips said?'

'Yes.'

'Was that all he said?'

You're well off, he had said, and you're dying of boredom. The baby's future, it seems to me, would be the least of your worries.

'More or less,' she said.

'Well, then, he's a fool.'

If you let her have an abortion she'll simply think the whole thing's dead easy and next year you'll have the same thing over again, only worse. Believe me, I know what I'm talking about.

'I thought you might be able to find out,' Angela insisted.

'That's why I came home. Otherwise, I wouldn't have bothered, would I? If I'd decided to have it, there wouldn't have been any point.'

After all, you are her mother. You've got to uphold a certain standard of decency. If you help her go through with this, you'll never be able to look her in the face again. You'll be putting yourself in the wrong and whatever she may feel now she'll never forgive you for it. Would you help her to steal? Good heavens, woman, would you advise her to commit murder?

'No,' she said. 'I'm glad you came. I mean, I'm glad you told me, but—'

'But what?' Angela asked, agonised. 'But what?'

'But nothing.'

It wasn't that she had taken a step; she had been pushed, stumbling forward and finding responsibility thrust into her arms, finding herself committed without knowing how it had happened. Because you couldn't stand still; because you couldn't follow from a distance, secretly caring; because there was no other way to go. 'It can't be so difficult,' she said. 'I'll do what I can. We'll—we'll fix it somehow.'

Unexpectedly—it should have been the other way round, she should have moved first—she was crushed in the long, bony arms, almost lifted off her feet.

'But you must promise,' she said breathlessly, 'not to do anything yourself. It might be dangerous.'

'I know. I won't. Thank you.'

'There's nothing to thank me for,' Ruth said. 'For heaven's sake, don't thank me.'

Angela stared at her for a moment, bewildered again. She herself felt light and free. Her mother looked to her quite old, angry and yet frightened. As she walked towards the door she seemed to stagger, give way, the exact motion of trying to carry something far too heavy.

'Are you all right? Has something happened? Shall I call that Beer woman?'

Ruth shook her head.

The chime of the gong sounded from the hall and before the last note had died away Rex was roaring, 'Are you ever coming? Is your mother coming down? Angela!'

'We're coming,' Angela shouted. She turned to Ruth, demanding, 'You aren't ill, are you?'

'No. Of course not.'

'Let's go, then. I suppose it's the strain or something. I'm absolutely ravenous.'

SATURDAY MORNING in Ramsbridge was panic-stricken, as though the following Sunday might last forever. Every butcher, fishmonger and baker had his nervous queue. Customers grasping lists made mental notes as they waited, of things they had forgotten in the last shop or must remember in the next; when they were pushed forward and spoken to by the raw-handed, bloody-aproned assistants they jumped to attention, stuttered, gabbled, their minds emptied of everything but the need for hurry. In Woolworth's a solid crowd churned like penned sheep between the high counters, the knee-level faces of bonneted children peering up to catch glimpses of paper streamers, icicles and holly, the Queen tinselled on a calendar as distant as the moon. The complaints and demands of the children, as though they were underground, were never heard. They tunnelled, tears and snot and iced lollies mixed to a thin glaze, between the huge haunches, occasionally stretching up a tentative hand to be slapped down with threats of murder by button-eyed, battling and winning Mums.

In the High Street three veterans were playing Ivor Novello very loudly and sadly on a cornet, a trumpet and a trombone. Their progress along the gutter was slower than funerals, their brazen moaning profitless. Cars were jammed nose to tail along both sides of the narrow streets, policemen bending and stepping slowly round them in a ritual dance, taking particulars, writing dozens of chits with the unhurried care of men who, balanced on the curb and in the middle of turmoil, record some inspiration. Already, in drapers' and stationers', locknit vests were labelled 'Acceptable Gift' and fountain pens sprouted holly, knicker elastic came in festive wrapping; great glossy annuals, a Boxing Day's reading, ousted year-old novels from the table marked 'New Books.' The cafés, dark little rooms furnished with brass and oak and gingham, were like dens of vice, reeling with blue smoke, deafening with chatter, an orgy of coffee and sugar buns, ice cream swimming in stemmed, metal dishes. Dogs snapped at cats, sleek from a week's window-dozing among the walnut layer cakes. Cerberus hat-stands groaned under caps and scarves, British warms and duffle-coats, riding macs, Tyrolean hombergs. Everything got lost, string gloves, walking-sticks, handbags, children. The cash registers rang like fire engines and the quiet, print-smocked waitresses snapped with the cold voices of women on the make.

It was in one of these cafés, The Plane Tree or The Tea Kettle that Angela had arranged for Tony to pick her up.

'He can't come home,' she said, 'because we can't talk with Daddy there.'

'I thought you were supposed to be ill,' Rex had snapped at Ruth. 'Too ill to go to Antibes, I'm told. Why the hell aren't you in bed?'

She was expected to be unstable, tears and laughter, a spring morning of a woman. So she giggled foolishly. 'Oh, but I'm better. I suppose it was just that I didn't want to go. That's what John said, anyway.'

He was angry; he was suspicious; he still believed that someone had been talking, but he had no proof. 'Oh, well,' he muttered, 'do what you like, I don't care. None of you have a v bloody gratitude. Lunatic asylum.' He went off to play f with Richard, sulking and mumbling like a child whose ans, impossible to reveal, have been upset.

'You are most certainly not going to drive the car,' Miss de Beer said. 'I never heard of such a thing—in your condition!'

'Why didn't you tell me?' Angela asked, with a bland gaze. 'Nobody ever tells me a thing.'

It was getting too much for Miss de Beer. She had everything packed to go to her sister's in Chelmsford. Now she had been asked to stay. Nobody thought of her as a human being. 'Oh!' she said, and slammed the baize door.

So, alarmed as a bird, dazed and incredulous, Ruth found herself in the Saturday morning fury of Ramsbridge. They had to walk the entire length of the High Street after parking the car, at the third attempt, outside the castellated, fortress-like public lavatories. Angela sloped along at her side, hands dug into the pockets of her black duffle-coat, stopping to look in jewellers' and ironmongers' windows while Ruth, handbag clutched like a shield, pushed on through the unyielding crowd. She was terrified. You know that the house creaks because of the dilation and contraction of wood; you know that the breathing in a darkened room is your own; you know that the ghost is a trick of light— but you are still terrified. She had never heard such noise, been so bludgeoned, so startled.

'It's Ruth. How are you, dear? I thought you'd gone off to Antibes.'

In spite of the length of this greeting and its formality, she took at least ten seconds to find, in the surrounding crowd, the tall, drooping, leather-clad Wilmington-Smiths.

'Hullo,' she said. 'No, I didn't go. How are you?' She was shoved from the back, side-stepped into the doorway of a shop.

'I did mean to come and see you when you were ill,' Meg said, 'but I've been having a simply ghastly time with the most horrid Swede. Edelgard left, you know.'

'Oh,' Ruth said. 'I'm sorry.'

She looked between them for Angela, saw her waiting on the other side of the pavement, leaning against a shooting brake and appearing, from her pursed lips, to be whistling.

'You know Angela,' she said desperately.

The door of the shop opened, disgorging three flustered women and a small crowd of children in camel-hair coats and knee socks; Ruth was flattened against the window in the attitude of someone standing on a high ledge. She tried, without being able to move, to summon Angela.

'Of course.' Childless themselves, they put on their child-loving smiles. Angela, as tall and lanky as they were, looked at them sullenly.

'How they grow,' Meg said, looking her once up and down.

'Yes,' Ruth breathed, 'don't they?'

'And how's Oxford?' John asked. 'Working hard?'

'Having a lovely time, I'm sure,' Meg said briskly. She was wondering, Ruth knew, why the girl didn't comb her hair or put on some decent clothes or stand straight or have a few manners. What would she think if she knew, if

Ruth said, 'She's pregnant and we are just going to meet the father of her child at The Tea Kettle Inn to talk about finding money for an abortion.' What, standing there in her pearls and her leather jacket and her crocheted hat, would she do? For a moment, backing towards the door, she had an insane temptation to find out. She swallowed and blinked, shaking her face into an uncertain smile.

'We just have to go in here for a moment. Lovely to see you, Meg. Good-bye.' She opened the door and slipped round it into the refuge of Baby Linen and Underwear. Angela followed stolidly.

'What was all that about?'

'I can't bear them.' She walked quickly, with purpose, up to the nearest counter.

'Why? They're all right. What's wrong with them?' Angela sat down on a high wooden chair, her black legs straddled, her face gloomy and patient. 'What do you want to buy in here, anyway?'

'Something for Jane's baby,' Ruth said.

'But you bought her that musical box.'

'It's not suitable,' Ruth snapped.

'Oh, well—' She got up and began wandering about.

Ruth, waiting, looked down through the glass-topped counter. Doesn't she realise, she asked herself violently? Doesn't she feel *anything?* But what do I expect her to do—cry, hide herself, keep apologising all the time? She was trembling with anger; but, like the fear, there was no reason for it. If I feel like this, she thought, I shall be no help to her. I've got to feel sorry for her. Whatever she does, whatever she says, I must feel sorry for her. She looked round with determination to call the girl back.

'Yes?' the assistant demanded. She looked about fourteen and sick to death of bootees and coloured safety-pins.

'I want,' Ruth said, searching the gloom at the back of the shop for Angela, 'something for a little girl of two.'

'What sort of thing?'

'Oh—' She snatched a blue animal from the counter and pressed it into the girl's hand. 'This'll do. I'll have this.'

She saw Angela wandering among the prams. She was alone there, meandering with vague, idle interest. An assistant went up to her and she shook her head. When she came back to Ruth, her long, shambling shape incongruous among women shoppers who looked at her with suspicion, she was grinning.

'Honestly,' she said, 'do I look as though I wanted to buy a pram? They must be crazy.'

'Come on,' Ruth rapped, in a dead voice. 'We're late.'

THEY SAT CRUSHED TOGETHER round the flimsy table, dodging the loaded hat-stand, staring at a minute urn of white heather in order to avoid looking at each other. Tony's chapped face and newly-combed centurion hair rose lugubriously out of the folds of his scarf. He had greeted them in a hushed voice and sunk back, as far as it was possible to sink back, into an attitude of reverent gloom. It was obviously not going to be necessary to impress on him the seriousness of the situation. He looked like a curate settling down to discuss dry-rot in the organ loft.

'Well,' Ruth said, 'let's get it over.'

Angela looked at her with mild surprise. Someone came to remove a duffle-coat from the hat-stand and they all three crouched forward over the white heather. Only Tony acknowledged the man's apologies. He believed, thank God, in good manners, whatever the crisis. When they sat back again he said in a low voice, 'Yes, well, it's very good of you, Mrs. Whiting—'

'Look,' Angela said. 'Do get the waitress.'

Tony made a few masterful, ineffectual gestures. A dog trailing a loose lead came and sniffed round his legs. He patted it briskly with his other hand. He was a man who could cope, thank God, with this sort of thing. 'Miss!' he said. 'Miss!'

'I do wish you wouldn't call waitresses Miss,' Angela grumbled. 'No wonder they never come.'

'We called them Miss at Harrow,' he said stiffly.

'Oh, well—' She sunk her chin on to her hand, rocking the table. The dog nosed at Ruth. She drew her legs up under the chair, but it followed them, snuffling and fawning.

'Please,' Ruth said, 'take the dog away.'

Tony reacted immediately, bending down, snapping his fingers, scrabbling for the dog's lead.

'Come on,' he said. 'Come on, boy. Out of there now, boy.'

The dog growled in the back of its throat, pressing its heavy, palpitating weight against Ruth's legs.

'Would you move, please?' the waitress asked tartly. 'I can't get by.'

'Can we have three coffees?' Angela said, looking up at the waitress.

'Come on, boy,' Tony muttered, tugging at the lead. 'Out you come, now.'

'I'm coming to you,' the waitress snapped. 'Would you mind moving, please?' .

Tony moved back an inch; the dog retreated; the lead tightened and the waitress stepped forward. She stumbled, spinning the tray like a conjurer in mid-air. For a moment, staring, horrified, upwards, Ruth imagined the slow descent of cups and saucers towards her, a cataclysm of coffee and china which would be in some way fatal, the end of everything. But the tray spun to a standstill, nothing was even spilt.

'There now!' the waitress blazed at Tony. 'See what you nearly did!'

'Can we have three coffees?' Angela repeated hopelessly.

'I'm *coming* to you,' the waitress hissed. The dog had slunk off, trailing its lead. On the other side of the room it lapped, with huge, noisy gulping, a bowl of tea. Someone else came to take his coat from the hat-stand. When it was all over, the crouching and moving and apologising, they again fastened their eyes, bright and dismayed, on the white heather.

'Well,' Ruth said, 'I suppose you've talked about this. I mean, I suppose you've talked about it before Angela came home.'

'Indeed,' Tony said. 'Naturally. And I would like to say at this point'—he looked up briefly—'how desperately sorry I am.'

Angela sighed through her nose, her elbow on the table, her lips pushed out like a sulky child. Ruth wanted to tell her to sit properly. She looked coldly at Tony.

'It's rather late for being sorry.'

'Yes, I know that, it's just that I would like you to appreciate—'

'Oh, do let's get this coffee,' Angela groaned. 'Honestly, we've been here for hours. Everyone knows we're sorry and all that. If you make a speech, I shall scream.'

'I didn't intend to make a speech as it happens.'

'Then don't.'

'Angela tells me that you want—that you have decided to get rid of the baby,' Ruth said. The waitress dumped down three cups of grey coffee.

'Biscuits?'

'No, thank you.'

'I'd like some biscuits,' Angela said. 'And we haven't got any sugar.'

'There's sugar in,' the waitress rapped, dashing away again.

'What happens if you don't take it?' Angela enquired. 'Really, what a ghastly place this is.'

'Well,' Tony said, 'I mean I don't see what else we can do really. Quite honestly, I mean. It's a terrible thing, I know, for Angela—'

'Yes. What are you going to do?'

'I'm sorry, I don't quite understand.'

'Do you know anyone? A doctor? Anyone?'

He was shocked, startled. 'I don't make a habit of this sort of thing, Mrs. Whiting. I'm really just as inexperienced as Angela. I believe there are ways and means, but I can't say I'm familiar with them.'

'He means,' Angela said, 'he doesn't know. He really doesn't. He only knows about that old woman with the catheter. Someone went to her once.'

'Biscuits,' the waitress announced, as though they were unrecognisable. A child of about eighteen months came staggering between the tables and stood, apparently transfixed, staring at Tony.

'Whassat?' it asked, pointing a wavering finger.

Tony smiled nervously. 'Yes,' he said, 'I believe there is a woman in Cowley—'

'Whassat? Whassat?'

'Oh, do go away,' Angela said vaguely. The child stepped nearer. It had thin orange hair, rheumy blue eyes and was zipped into scarlet tartan.

'Ullo,' it wheedled. 'Whassat?'

'Oh, for God's sake,' Angela said, plunging her head between her hands. 'Do go *away*.'

'There's no point in talking like that,' Ruth muttered. She got up and took the child's hand, cold and lifeless as a doll's hand. Edging the child in front of her, she pushed between the tables. Nobody seemed to recognise it and the child seemed to have no views. Seated in the bay window were five young women, one with red hair.

'Is this your child?' Ruth asked hesitantly.

The young woman looked round in the middle of laughing. Her face stiffened and she said aggressively, 'Yes, of course she's my child. Why? Was she annoying you?'

'No, of course not.'

'Well, then, what's the matter?'

'Nothing. It was just that she was—wandering about.'

'She always wanders about. Can you think of any reason why she shouldn't?' Her hostility was alarming. 'Most people,' she said, 'don't mind a small child wandering about, but of course if she was being a nuisance—'

'No,' Ruth said.

'It really seems to me,' the young woman said, glancing triumphantly at her friends, 'that you might mind your own business.'

'Whassat?' the child demanded.

'It's a cigarette lighter,' a young woman explained coldly. 'For lighting cigarettes with. Why don't you go and talk to that nice dog over there?'

When Ruth got back to the table both Angela and Tony were looking flushed and sullen. They had obviously been quarrelling and the foolishness, the futility of this had not occurred to either of them. When Ruth sat down they remained stony, immovable.

108

'We aren't getting anywhere,' Ruth said.

'You don't say,' Angela mumbled.

'But we've got to get somewhere. There isn't so very much time.'

'Well, there is this woman in Cowley. And I've got a friend who says he'd give her an injection. Of course that wouldn't cost anything, which is quite a point.'

'Is it?' Ruth demanded. She swallowed the desire to shout, to rush out into the air, to burst into reckless tears. 'Would you be happy for her to go to some woman in Cowley or let your friend give her an injection? Would you?'

'Well,' he said uneasily, 'I know it's not very pleasant, but after all—'

Angela looked frightened. 'After all what?' she asked.

'Well. I mean, well, what else is there? Perhaps you know of someone, Mrs. Whiting?'

It was not, perhaps, meant viciously, but it was the first point he had scored. His cold, already ageless eyes held Ruth's for a moment. She recognised them as the eyes of a man who felt nothing. Posturing for other people, for the countless mirrors, he would assume attitudes of outrage, love, friendship, even physical need. He would probably go through his entire life imagining that he was real; but not one person would owe him gratitude, remember his comfort. At the moment, still so young, he didn't even know what he was meant to be feeling. The attitude was uncertain, but the intention was clear: I shall never do anything for anyone, because I don't believe anyone except myself exists. There was no shaking it, no changing it. It was useless to try.

'No,' Ruth said wearily, 'I don't know of anyone. But

I've told Angela that I'll try to find out. She is not going to any woman in Cowley. I hope that's quite clear to both of you.'

They said nothing. Ruth repeated sharply, 'Do you understand?'

'Of course,' Tony said, 'if you can find some better way.'

'It will be expensive.'

'Yes, well of course I wanted to talk to you about that, I—'

She said wildly, 'It will be at least a hundred pounds.'

'Perhaps I can borrow a hundred pounds.'

'Who from?' Angela asked, incredulous.

'I don't see that that matters,' he said stiffly.

'But who? Who on earth has a hundred pounds?'

'Plenty of people.'

'Who? Your father?'

'Of course not!' he said indignantly. 'I wouldn't dream of telling my father!'

'Why not? It was you who told me to tell my mother.'

'That's different. You haven't told your father.'

'I thought your father was supposed to be so jolly progressive and everything. I thought—'

'Oh, shut up!' he said brutally. 'Do stop nattering at me.'

'Well, really, I suppose it's you who's got to go through all this, I suppose it's me who's telling you to go to that filthy old woman—'

Ruth stood up, knocking back her chair.

'Check?' the waitress asked hopefully.

'I'll have it,' Tony said. He slammed sixpence on the table and stamped over to the cash desk.

Ruth turned desperately to Angela.

'You don't have to go back with him now,' she said.

'I'll drive you back this afternoon. I've got nothing else to do. You really don't have to go with him.'

'Why?' Angela asked calmly, turning up her coat collar. 'I mean, that's silly when he's come all this way to fetch me. Besides, it's more fun on the Vespa.'

'But—'

'You aren't *worrying* about me, are you?' Angela asked, grinning suddenly as she had in the shop. 'You don't think it would be *bad* for me, do you? Because that would be too funny for words.'

'No,' Ruth said. 'It's not that.'

'Well, will you let me know what happens? I suppose if he can borrow a hundred pounds it'll be all right, won't it? I must say I can't imagine who's going to lend it to him, but still.'

'Well, good-bye then,' Ruth said.

'Aren't you coming out?'

'No, I'm just going to—to the Ladies'. Good-bye, darling.'

The cool cheek, the cold hair, were pressed against hers. 'You've been super. I knew you would be. Thanks awfully.'

'You promise not to—do anything silly?'

'Of course. 'Bye now. See you soon.'

She hurried out, pushing impatiently through the crowd; the door slammed and rang behind her. Ruth sat down again at the empty table. There was no Ladies' Room in The Tea Kettle Inn. She waited, staring at the white heather which swelled and blurred and streamed away like a white cloud, long after the roar of the Vespa had grown and died in the street outside.

Chapter 18

No!' JANE GASPED. Her eyes and mouth made three perfect rounds, like an advertisement for some particularly succulent sweet. '*What* a silly girl!'

'Yes,' Ruth said. A lifetime of keeping secrets had made this confidence so painful that she had hardly believed it would be possible. She had brought the blue animal and now picked it up, tempted to wonder what it was, tweaked its unidentifiable ears. 'The point is,' she said, 'what are we going to do about it?'

'She's going to get rid of it, of course?'

'Well, yes.'

'You don't sound very certain.'

'I'm not.'

'But you don't seriously think she could *have* it, do you?'

'No. No, of course I don't.'

'Well, that's a relief anyway. For one ghastly moment I thought you were brooding about the layette.' She got up from the armchair, into which she had plumped with horror, and started to bustle about the room. Jane often bustled about the room, suddenly remembering to stir her life, as though it were kept simmering on a low flame. When this was done, with nothing apparently achieved, she came back and sat by the fire, her arms clasped round her knees.

'Does Rex know?'

'No. He was furious about me not going away, but I think John Phillips talked him round. I mean, I don't think he thinks it's anything to do with Angela.'

'You don't want him to know, of course. He'd blow the roof off.'

'He wouldn't understand,' Ruth said cautiously.

'No, I can see that. Well, do you know anyone?'

'That's why I came. John won't have anything to do with it—'

'You mean you asked him?'

'Yes. I mean it seems so obvious, doesn't it?' Then she added hopelessly, 'I suppose it doesn't. What I came to ask was, do you know of anyone?'

'Heavens, I used to. There was some Irishman, Susan Raynes said he was a real angel. Richard would probably know. I could 'phone him. Then Yvonne used to swear by some man in Chelsea somewhere. She's tried Epsom salts, I suppose, and all that?'

'No,' Ruth said. 'I don't think so.'

'Well, do tell her. You never know. And there's something you can put on cotton wool, and I believe there's a special sort of soap—'

'No,' Ruth said.

She could not explain to Jane, to anyone, least of all to Angela, how she felt. A woman may have a son of fifty, bald, paunchy, with a roll of fat at the back of his neck and hands that sweat like putty; or a daughter, old, the arthritic legs and dripping nose blurting out failure, a grey bag of wasted muscles and gangling bones. Bone of your bones; curious flesh of your flesh. Not a hair, not a fingernail, not a particle of skin is the same as it was at the moment of birth, but still the ageing body that was once a child is part of you. You may not understand a word it says, may be baffled or gratified or hostile; the physical substance of the child is still, though changed beyond recognition, your own.

So to Ruth it was a sense of personal, physical outrage that made her so violently opposed to pills and soaps, sharp instruments prodded with old women's hands. Angela herself might not have minded. After all, it happened to plenty of girls who, according to the law, were fit and willing to become mothers. It was unreasonable to try and preserve some remnant of innocence.

'No,' she repeated strongly. 'It's got to be done properly. I couldn't bear it to be like that.'

Jane looked at her sharply. 'I suppose it'll have to be done the way you can get it done. It's not exactly a question of choosing, is it?'

Ruth got up and wandered restlessly across the room.

'Where's Baby?'

'Asleep. I drugged her.'

'Did you have anyone down for the weekend?'

'No. I had her the whole solid time. She hits me now. She's vicious. I say, what an extraordinary thought—you'd be a grandmother. How very sinister.'

'Yes,' Ruth said. She leapt away, ran to the most remote distance. "I had a letter from that girl you had staying here, Maxine.'

'Ah. Maxine.' Jane shot out of her chair. 'Now *she* would know. Why don't you ask her?'

'Ask her? About Angela?'

'Of course. Why don't you ring her up? I've got her number here somewhere.'

'But I couldn't just ring her up like that—'

'Why not?' Jane's hands flew about among the papers and toys and beads and magazines, pounced at last on her address book. She looked at Ruth. 'All right, then. I will. Do you want me to?'

Ruth nodded slowly. Jane dialled the operator and settled herself in the armchair. With her free hand she reached for a newly-sharpened pencil and a sheet of paper.

'But don't you remember,' Ruth said, 'she agreed with *Rex*—'

Jane beat her down impatiently and asked for the number. Ruth sat down in the corner of the room. She felt tired and confused, as incapable as Angela of assuming the right attitude. If she answers, she thought superstitiously, it will mean I'm right; if she doesn't, I'm wrong.

'Hullo?' Jane said. 'Is that you, Herb? Jane, here. No, Jane Tanner . . . How is all? What are you up to—?'

For what seemed an interminable time, he told her what he was up to. Jane laughed regularly, gasped with surprise, drew neat designs on the sheet of paper.

'Well,' she said at last, 'isn't that exciting. Is Maxine there? Could I have a tiny word with her? Bless you—' She nodded encouragingly at Ruth, then piped up, 'Maxine, love. How is all? What have you been up to—?'

Already the complexities of feeling, the fear, the reluctance, had disappeared. It was all as gay as a bridge party, as slick as exchanging hairdressers.

'I'm so out of touch down here and I thought you might possibly know . . . A friend of mine, the silly girl, is in a fix, you know how it is . . . Well, rather urgent really—'

Ruth tried to imagine Maxine on the other end of the line, and failed. She could only summon up an absurd vision of someone in black satin, inhaling the telephone and lying down to do it.

'Yes?' Jane was saying, the pencil poised. 'Of course I won't breathe a word ... Stein like in the thing you drink out of? No, I said is it Stein, S-T-E-I-N? ... Fickstein? Ah, I get it: 38 Rowntree House ... Where is that? ... You are an angel, I'll tell her to get on to him right away ... Yes, I understand that, I'll tell her ... That sounds absolutely marvellous. Just the job ... No, I quite agree with you, personally I hate the whole business, but sometimes it just can't be helped, can it?'

Her voice trotted on, pausing now and then, taking small detours round the subject, busy and ferreting. She underlined the name Fickstein several times and decorated it with elaborate trelliswork. Ruth got up and looked at the book-shelf. It was largely filled with textbooks on the rearing of children. Because she did not want to look as though she were waiting, because she wanted, now, to assume some kind of worldly indifference, she pulled out a book, opened it, stared at it intently.

'Well, I *know*,' Jane was saying, 'do you know Betty Rickworth? She's just had to adopt one, they absolutely ruined her—'

'The growing child,' Ruth found herself reading, 'more than repays his parents for their pains. Does he not renew and preserve their youth, cement their marriage, refresh their minds, and offer them their fair share or more of vicarious immortality? "He that regardeth the wind shall not sow" and it is doubtful whether most of us have either the wisdom or the knowledge to justify us in carefully planning our children's births—'

'Oh, I think she's much better ... No, she didn't go to

Antibes . . . No, she hasn't gone . . . I don't know why'—an unusual edge of coldness had come into Jane's voice—'I suppose she didn't want to . . . Well, a million thanks, we'll contact Doctor Fickstein . . . No, it's nobody here. What? On the *Common!* We just drown them here, along with the puppies . . . Good-bye, love, and thank you again—'

She put down the receiver and tapped her teeth with the end of the pencil.

'Strange,' she said. 'Now how did she know you were going to Antibes?'

'She knew someone?'

'Yes. A Doctor Fickstein. She says not to be put off by the name, he's perfectly sweet and does the whole thing almost legally, it's all very smart and painless and will cost the earth. What a curious girl that is. Anyway, there you are.' She handed Ruth the sheet of paper. 'She says not to mention her on any account, but if he wants to know who sent you, say Mrs. Baltimore. It doesn't sound very likely, somehow.'

'Is she Mrs. Baltimore? Maxine?'

'Who knows? You'd better ring him up and make an appointment.' She got up and bustled for a few seconds in front of the fire. 'You're all right?' she asked. 'I mean, apart from all this?'

'Yes. I'm all right now.'

'And how's the dreadful de Beer?'

'She's leaving on Friday. I can't bear her watching me all the time. She listens at doors.'

'But Rex doesn't know she's going?'

'No. Not yet.'

'Quite right,' Jane said shortly. 'Anyone who tells Rex anything is asking for trouble.'

'Oh, I don't know—' She evaded the subject of Rex, pushing the book back into the shelf, folding the piece of paper and holding it inside her pocket.

'I never noticed before. Just then you looked exactly like Angela. I mean, not that you do. You just looked like her.'

'I must go,' Ruth said quickly.

'Oh, don't go, Meg and Lorna are coming in. Meg says that Betty knocked poor old Robert down the stairs the other day because he missed the 5.50. If that's the sort of welcome he gets I should think he'll miss it for good. I can't think why she wants him home every night. The bliss of Mondays, being able to stretch out in bed.'

Ruth looked at her as she chattered, small and fat and apparently contented, with her adored, drugged child and her husband satisfactorily in London. She could imagine the three women sprawled out over the furniture like men, chipping at each other with small, delicate hammers. She could imagine the cigarettes burning down to last weekend's nail varnish, the kicked-off shoes, the finishing of Richard's whisky. Long after midnight Meg and Lorna, with groans, would wrap themselves up, get into their cars with cries of farewell and drive off in opposite directions to their electrically heated, empty beds. Time would have passed. Time would have been killed. Only thirty living days till Christmas.

'What did you say?' Jane asked.

'I said no, I must go.'

'I thought you said something about Christmas.'

'It's near, isn't it? The boys will be home in about three weeks. I hadn't realised.'

'You'd better get on with it. You can't spend your time arranging abortions in the middle of all those paper hats and crackers and so on. You'll have to tell Fickstein to hurry.'

'I know.'

She walked home along the lane. The moonlight turned the garden ash-grey, ashen grass stretching out to the darker shrubbery. The grey gravel swerved up to the house like a river, each pebble glistening. She walked on the edge of the grass, silently approaching the house as though, if startled, it might spring on her.

The front door opened as she crept on to the step.

'There you are,' Miss de Beer said, catching her out. 'I waited up for you.'

'You shouldn't have done,' Ruth said faintly, stepping inside.

'I owe it to Mr. Whiting,' Miss de Beer said. 'Mr. Whiting telephoned and I said you were with Mrs. Tanner.'

'Thank you.'

'I took the opportunity of telling Mr. Whiting that you had given me notice.'

Ruth paused on the stairs. She looked down, as though searching for Miss de Beer in the unaccustomed brightness.

'What did he say?'

'Naturally, he said that you were not fit enough to be left alone. He asked me to overlook what you had said, and to stay on until your daughter comes back from Oxford.'

'Very well. Good-night, Miss de Beer.'

'There is a thermos of Ovaltine in your room, and I've put out your sleeping pill. It is very difficult for me to stay where I'm not wanted.' As Ruth was slowly ascending the stairs, she raised her voice with each word to carry a little farther.

'I'm sorry,' Ruth said.

She closed the bedroom door. The room was warm and comforting. She took the piece of paper out of her pocket, smoothed it open, read the name and address over again. She knew by now that Miss de Beer went through her drawers, read all her letters, listened in to most of her telephone calls. She thought of putting the paper under her pillow; but if she forgot to take it out before de Beer made the bed? If she put it in one of her drawers, or pockets, de Beer would certainly find it while she was having her bath. Where does one hide things? She looked urgently round the room. Under the carpet, in a shoe, in a hatbox? She folded the paper very small and tucked it under the blue silk coverlet of the musical box. She did not, as she was tempted to do, turn the handle, but tapped the fragile cradle twice with her finger. It rocked a few times, and stood still.

Chapter 19

THE BEGINNING of the day: they are all fallen in their beds as though the attack of sleep had been so sudden that they had no time to fold their hands, point their feet upwards in a more seemly imitation of death.

Rex lies on his back. His mouth is open as though he is being forcibly fed with air. One arm is flung across his own chest—he might have been struck down while trying to keep warm.

Maxine, turned away from him, sleeps like a child who has fallen asleep on the floor and been carried, compact and motionless, to bed. Her arm is under her head, for a pillow, the fat flesh of her cheek pushed upwards; her lips blow open, fall shut, as imperceptibly as the breathing of a medusa, a living plant.

He wanted love. Why shouldn't he have love? She thought he was attractive, generous; even witty. She laughed at his jokes. He knew they weren't good jokes; so did she, but she laughed at them.

Well, that's what I mean by love. I know I'm fat and she knows I'm fat; but she says goodness, I think you've got a fine figure, really I do, I hate those scrawny men like Herb. That could be more tactfully said, perhaps, but it's the lie that matters—the love.

Oh, God, it's the lies one wants. She's a good liar. Oh, Rex, I feel perfectly awful, really I do, you've got such a sweet wife but I just feel you need me, that's all, and if I feel anyone needs me well, I just can't help it, I just can't stop myself . . . Oh, Rex.

Silly little fool. Silly, uncomplicated fool. Tell me I'm young, Maxine, tell me I'm a success, tell me everyone loves me. Tell me I'm nice, Maxine. Go on. Tell me I'm nice.

Pliable, not a bone in her conscience, she does it. Gratitude softens his face as he sleeps. The open mouth slackens into a smile of relief.

Ruth? Ruth? He whimpers, this heavy ageing man; wakes with his mouth drawn down at the corners as though he is about to cry. It is grey and cold and Friday. He turns, his stomach falling like a loose, heavy sack between himself and Maxine. He hasn't the courage to wake her. He lies looking at the back of her head, uncomforted.

Angela sleeps in her cell, her room which should be gay with cushions or theatre programmes or comic pottery, but isn't. The distant clocks have been chiming and ringing all night to pass the time. She lies on her stomach, to hide or protect time, one arm hanging over the edge of the bed, her head wrenched sideways.

Everything about her now is unformed. Her intelligence has stopped working. She is herself and, as she flounders, flies, sinks from one dream to another, unrecognisable.

What does myself look like? I mean, who am I?

You are an examination result, dear. Perhaps, in time, a scholarship. Perhaps an honours degree. Try harder.

But myself—I mean myself?

Perhaps you could find yourself in the Guides, or in the

New Testament somewhere. If not, we can provide various substitutes, such as Joan of Arc, Florence Nightingale, Nurse Cavell. It's really none of our business, but we do keep a few heroines handy, just in case.

But how shall I deal with myself? What shall I do with myself all my life?

You may look in the answer book. You must control yourself, discipline yourself, sacrifice yourself, respect yourself. If necessary you may defend yourself and abase yourself, and to have confidence in yourself while effacing yourself is not entirely bad. You must never, however, love yourself or pity yourself, praise yourself or allow yourself to have either will or opinion. Never indulge yourself, never be conscious of yourself, never forget yourself and, above all, never be centred in yourself. We hope this is understood?

But if there is no one else to love, pity or praise? If no one else is conscious of me, remembers me, if I am no one's centre?

That, dear, is what God is for. As Our Lord said, 'Are not five sparrows sold for two farthings and not one of them is forgotten before God?' To forget yourself in one sense is desirable, whereas, as we have said, to forget yourself in another sense is not. Now if we rewrite these subjoined sentences, strengthening them by the omission of caveats, trite quotations, indirect assertions and vulgarisms everything, we feel certain, will seem a great deal clearer; or, alternatively, more clear.

She twists her head, hitting the mattress with a vague, feeble gesture. 'But I'll never get there,' she says, stating a proved fact. 'I'll never get there.'

The clocks repeat themselves. She turns on to her back

and, still asleep, rubs her stomach with the unhappy, worried expression of a child who has eaten a sour apple.

Jane Tanner reads.
'Tabitha Twitchit kept the only other shop in the village. She did not give credit.'
'Why?'
'Ginger and Pickles gave unlimited credit.'
'Read it. Go on.'
'Now the meaning of "credit" is this—'
'Don't go to sleep. Read it. Go on.'
'When a customer buys a bar of soap, instead of the customer pulling out a purse and paying for it, she says—'
'What are you crying for? Did you bite your tongue?'

A white fog rolls over the Common, the air of this new day has never felt the sun. Betty Johnson, asleep, is jealous of her husband's dreams. He is dreaming of playing cricket on his own lawn. Miss de Beer hears a bell and struggles to answer it. 'It's for Father,' she says, and loses track, dismayed in her sleep by her forgetfulness.

Chapter 20

IN THE HALF-DARK, Ruth couldn't find the alarm clock. Its ringing seemed to fill the house. At last she knocked it over, stifled it. The air was cold as cellars and she shivered as she pulled on her clothes, her breath clouded the mirror as she peered to put on her hat. Dressed in suit, hat and overcoat she padded about the room in stockinged feet, an odd, top-heavy figure scuttling silently backwards and forwards for things she had almost forgotten—lipstick, cheque book, handkerchief, comb, purse, car keys, Doctor Fickstein's address from the musical box. She opened the door by inches and, holding her shoes, crept along the landing. Her feeling of foolishness—a grown woman escaping from her own house—turned to excitement. Her heart thumped, her muscles tightened with the pleasurable terror of a child in hiding. The stairs creaked and the kitchen door whined on its hinges. She noticed that although Miss de Beer had nobly waited up for her the night before, she hadn't washed the supper dishes. The kitchen smelt sourly of old meals. The tiles were like ice under her feet and she stumbled over Rex's gum boots, which he wore when talking to the gardener. She waited for a moment, holding her breath, then stepped over the boots and unbolted the back door. The mist swirled in, damping the tiled floor, the gibbeted macintoshes, the muddy gum boots askew in the middle of the passage. She left the door open, partly out of malice towards Miss de Beer and partly to air the kitchen; then she tiptoed painfully over the sharp gravel and into the dank, petrol-smelling garage.

It was impossible to open the garage doors silently; but by now, even if she was heard, it would be too late. She put on her shoes, pushed the doors back and got into the car. The engine coughed, stuttered and died. She pulled out the choke and rammed her foot on the accelerator. The engine gave a loud, asthmatic moan and shuddered to silence. She was now really frightened, her mouth open with horror. She imagined Miss de Beer storming into the garage in her candlewick dressing-gown, her hair in armour, wrenching her out of the car, telephoning Rex, telephoning John Phillips . . . She flattened her thumb against the self-starter, bore down with all her weight on the accelerator; disagreeable, hacking and hawking and racking like an old man, the efforts were deafening. She swore, whispering. Then she sat back and, her hands loose on the clammy steering-wheel, counted ten. There was no sound anywhere but the dripping of the mist from the bushes. She switched off the engine and waited.

After ten slow seconds she turned the key gently, pressed the starter button with the palm of her hand, caressing it. The deep snore of the engine immediately filled the garage. She smiled gratefully, letting out her breath in a puff of relief. Reversing into the drive she saw the lit square of Miss de Beer's window and an agitated figure wrestling to open it. She put her hand out of the car and waved cheerfully, keeping her hand fluttering as she swerved away down the drive.

The elation lasted almost until she got to Ramsbridge. The feeling of foolishness returned slowly, drab as toothache. Why hadn't she just told Miss de Beer she was going to London, firmly, with dignity? Because she would have to have thought of a reason. Why? What right had the woman got to demand reasons? Because she was employed by Rex to be, in her own words, a companion: someone who accompanies the sick, or aged, or harmlessly insane, removes razor blades and shoelaces out of reach and is always on the holding end of the knitting wool. She would have been right to demand a reason; that was what she was paid for. And if a convincing lie could have been thought of, she would probably have insisted on coming too. She parked the car in the station yard and fell in with the anxious, bleeding, unbuttoned straggle of commuters.

By the time the train wound into Paddington the sky over the slag heaps was clear, winter blue and she had realised, as reason threatened to make even the purpose of her journey uncertain, that Miss de Beer would have already telephoned Rex. She had no idea what to do about this, except to try and avoid thinking about it. She half expected to see him, glowering and handsome and portly in his light-grey overcoat, waiting for her on the platform. She jumped out of the train and hurried across to the taxi rank, hugging her coat round her in the queue, keeping her head down like a diffident, muffled spy.

'Hullo, Ruth. You're early this morning.' Robert Johnson paused in mid-stride, walked two steps backwards, a hurrying man stopped short and reversed on film. His eyes looked liquid and sad under the black Homburg and, as usual, he had cut himself shaving.

'Oh. Hullo, Robert.' She couldn't think of anything else to say.

'Waiting for a taxi?'

'Yes. Yes, I am.'

'Dreadfully cold down there this morning, wasn't it?'

'Yes, freezing.' She stamped her feet, furtively moving along the queue, to reassure him how remarkably cold it was. He took another step backwards, still facing the end of the platform as though to prove that he was on his way, and that this was no assignation.

'I didn't see you on the train.'

'No. I didn't see you either.'

'Well, it's the tube for me. You get there, you know, much quicker in the end.' His melancholy look, his tired voice, gave a sad profundity to the remark. Where, she found herself wondering, and what end? Poor Robert, haunted by lechery. She smiled at him warmly.

'I expect you do,' she said.

He blushed, and switched his umbrella and brief-case from hand to hand. 'Well,' he said, 'we must all meet some time.'

'Yes, we must.' She jostled forward. He put himself into gear and leapt off down the platform. 'Have a good day,' she called, foolhardy. He waved his umbrella without turning, a man going over the top.

What did he think she was up to? Probably, conditioned as he was, he imagined a tryst in Swiss Cottage, a lover in Finchley. She felt a short moment of regret that this wasn't so; that the significance of the day was not hers, but Angela's. She could have asked Robert to lunch with her.

Why not? Perhaps, she thought, cheerful again, I am really a little mad. She stepped into the taxi like a busy, pretty woman stepping into a taxi, conscious of mincing, the skirt tightened round her thighs, neat and alluring and a little smug.

Chapter 21

S HE LOOKED CURIOUSLY out of the window as they crawled along Praed Street and the Edgware Road. Safe in the taxi, she fastened on the crowds, the bicycles hung up in shops like meat, the nudes outside the Metropole, the barrows and mop-haired boys in black ties and perilous bus conductors and old women nipping on and off like crows: anything to postpone Doctor Fickstein, the thought of Rex, the realisation of what she was actually doing. Maida Vale loomed empty, no one in the streets but solitary policemen and errand boys weaving lazily on their bicycles round the genteel, dejected crescents. She pulled off her gloves and put them on again, moistened her lips, held her purse ready. Up the hill, stopping at the lights for one small child on a tricycle to pedal carefully by, through a maze of roads where detached houses cold-shouldered each other behind high walls and side gates were marked Trademan's Entrance. She peered at the meter and counted out two shillings more. Her watch said five to eleven, but she couldn't remember when she had last put it right. Did it gain or lose? She shook her wrist, listened in case the watch had stopped. They were in a town of new buildings, unrecognisable, high, narrow blocks of flats arranged haphazardly together like building blocks tumbled out of a sack.

Their height excluded the sun, but the patches of grass in front of them were bright green, like dyed raffia.

'Rowntree House?' the driver asked, leaning back as though reining in his taxi.

'Yes.' She glanced at the crumpled paper.

He peered about a little, crawling along in the street that seemed to have been stricken by plague; not a cat or a dog, nothing but the thousands of muslin-curtained eyes staring down on the creeping, ant-sized taxi. He turned in through a gateway, drew up outside an enormous portico with double doors twenty feet high.

'Well,' he said. 'Here it is.'

Ruth paid him, hesitating until he had driven off, rollicking away into the common sun of London. She wondered how she would ever get away again, imagined herself wandering the canyon streets till nightfall. She pushed nervously at the door, which gave way without a sound. A small, pale commissionaire got up from his chair and enquired softly, 'Yes, madam?'

She saw, in the dimness, a vast, marble-floored hall. The two chairs put, for some reason, in the middle of it were like thrones for midgets. There was a strange sound of dripping water. Great urns, weeping maidenhair fern and carnations, stood about as though in preparation for some ghoulish wedding. She jumped, clutching her handbag in both hands.

'Number 38?' she whispered, then repeated loudly, 'Number 38, please.'

'Doctor Fickstein?'

She nodded.

'Across the hall there, the lift is through the door on the left, it's on the first floor.'

'Thank you.'

She stepped off the carpet on to the marble. A shallow, oblong pool accounted for the dripping water; the water was clear but the fish, rolling from side to side, looked dead. One side of the hall was lined with prams of various sizes and shapes, push chairs and children's tricycles. Some were shrouded in rugs or plastic covers; they looked as though they were stored against the possibility of children who would never come, like bath chairs in a disused pump-room.

The hall was a folly, the result of a short period of madness. Behind it, through a swing door there was a warren of narrow corridors, hardly wide enough to walk without sidling. The lift was a space rocket in which, with some manipulation and difficulty, it was just possible to raise her arm from the elbow to press the button. When the doors automatically slid back she found herself on a dark landing, a kind of balcony hanging over the lift shaft. There was complete silence and almost complete darkness. She had no matches and it was impossible to see the numbers on the doors. She stood near the wall, looking from side to side, uncertain what to do, ready to jump back into the lift. The lift sank swiftly away and simultaneously all the lights came on. She pressed the bell of Number 38.

After a slow minute, the door was opened by a white-coated receptionist. The flat seemed to have been designed to withstand seige. She led Ruth through three hallways, each increasing in size but each windowless. After crossing them, she closed the doors firmly. There were then two intercommunicating rooms which had no apparent purpose, being without any form of furniture which could be used for sitting, lying or putting things on; there were plenty of clocks, knickknacks, vases of pampas grass, pedestals, mirrors framed in mother-of-pearl, but again no windows. When the receptionist ushered Ruth into the final room, daylight came as a surprise. The receptionist turned on all the lamps, their stands green glass, china decorated with dragons, their shades all draped and tasselled silk. Then she went away, closing the doors behind her.

I want to get out. I'm trapped. Why am I doing this? Oh, I want to get out. Ruth walked quickly towards the door, then turned and walked back to the window. Her heels rapped on the parquet floor, agitated in the silence. She sat down on a small gilt chair, picked up a French fashion magazine, looked at it blankly, dropped it again. At least it isn't squalid.

She wasn't sure whether she had spoken out loud and pressed her lips firmly together. If you keep your mouth shut, she used to tell Angela when she cried, the sound can't come out. Julian and Mike had been allowed to howl, except by Rex, who said she was bringing them up to be a couple of pansies. What would they think of this? Nothing. They wouldn't know what to think. Jolly bad luck, what a clot she is. I say, my sister's had an abortion, she nearly died actually. I say, Whiting's sister had an abortion, he says she nearly died. I say, Whiting's mother made his sister have an abortion and she died. . . .

'Stop it,' she whispered. She would have welcomed anyone, even Miss de Beer. Even, bursting through the fortress doors, tracked her down, found her out, finished with her for good, Rex.

'Doctor Fickstein will see you now.'

She gathered up her gloves and handbag, cleared her throat. 'Thank you.'

Chapter 22

W HAT'S THE TIME?' Angela asked.
'You've asked me six times during the last half hour.'

'Well, what is it?'

'It's about five minutes later than it was before.'

'Oh, for heaven's sake, it's not so *difficult* to look at your watch, is it?' She leant over and roughly pulled back Tony's sleeve. He pulled his wrist away, slumped back in the huge leather armchair.

'It's ten to eight. That means that in ten minutes it'll be eight o'clock.' He looked quickly round the almost empty lounge. 'Can't you stop nattering?'

'I'm not nattering.'

'At least if we've got to sit here we might have a drink.'

'Oh, all right, all right!' she snapped, whispering. She dug in her handbag and pulled out a ten-shilling note, throwing it down on the table. 'Have a drink, then.'

'If that's your attitude, I wouldn't dream of it.'

She shrugged, looking away from him and the money.

'What did you say?' he asked hopefully.

'I didn't say anything.'

'Oh, really, Angela, you're becoming impossible.' He turned his back on her, disassociating himself. Somebody came in through the revolving doors and the ten-shilling note lifted and drifted on to the carpet. Neither of them moved to pick it up but watched it, warily, out of the corners of their eyes.

'You don't have to sit here,' Angela said. 'I'm quite capable of making a telephone call by myself, you know.'

'If I didn't,' he muttered, 'you'd say I didn't care.'

'Well, you don't, do you? Just sitting here doesn't make any difference.'

'Oh, shut up.'

They sat in silence. At the other end of the lounge, deeply embedded in a leather sofa, a boy and a girl were whispering to each other. They peered at each other's faces with the myopia of love. They breathed each other's breath. They were gentle, as though they were already very old.

'Don't let's quarrel,' Angela said humbly. 'I'm sorry.'

'Good heavens, you're the only one who's quarrelling.'

'I'm not. I'm not, honestly.'

'It's eight o'clock. Why don't you ring up and get it over?'

'All right. Will you come with me?'

'There isn't room in the box.'

She got up, picked up the ten-shilling note and handed it to him. 'Will you buy us a drink, then?' Trying to smile, to look appealing, to be loved. He nodded and took the money, forgiving her.

Crushed into the telephone booth while the operator got the number, she watched him summon the waiter, sitting back in the chair like a man in a club, a man of wealth. She heard the operator say, 'Miss Angela Whiting is calling you from a call box in Oxford and wishes you to—' Then there was a click and silence. Two girls crossed the foyer and stopped to talk to Tony, obscuring him with their stiff skirts and plump, bare shoulders.

'Hullo? Angela?' The voice was very far away.

'Hullo—' The two girls had sat down, spreading their skirts, balancing on the edge of their seats with their small feet arranged tidily beneath them. Angela turned her back on them. 'Hullo,' she repeated gruffly. 'Did you—did you see him?'

'Yes. I saw him.'

'Well, what did he say?' The line seemed dead. 'Hullo? Are you there?'

'I'm sorry.' Her mother sounded shrill, taut, as though her voice was being played at the wrong speed. 'I only just got in. I didn't expect you to ring so early.'

'It's eight o'clock.'

'Is it?'

'What did he *say?* Did you fix anything?'

'Hang on a minute, will you?' There was the sound of the receiver being put down on the table. Angela turned and looked through the glass door. The waiter was bending, putting glasses on the table, waiting for Tony to take the ten-shilling note from his wallet. The two girls raised their glasses, simpering, saying, 'Cheers.' Tony was drinking beer. A man's drink. Hatred or love, whichever it was, made her feel suddenly sick.

'Hullo?' she insisted. 'Hullo?'

'Yes. I'm here.' The voice was calmer now. 'It's all going to be all right, but we've got to find a doctor.'

'What do you mean? I thought you'd found one. I mean, Fickstein's a doctor, isn't he?'

'Yes, but a—an ordinary doctor has to write a letter

saying that he thinks it's necessary for you to—that you can't—'

'But why?'

'And then you have to go to a psychiatrist, so they can say you aren't—you know, mentally fit or something—' The voice broke down again. Tony was offering cigarettes to the two girls.

'Mummy? Mummy, are you there?'

'Yes. Look, it's difficult to explain on the telephone—'

'But we've got to decide! Did you tell him that? I mean, did you tell him it's urgent?'

'Of course. But this is the only way.'

'It isn't the only way! I could have it done tomorrow, without all this fuss. And I think,' she struggled with words and tears like a child, 'I think I jolly well will!'

'Angela—'

She should have slammed down the receiver. She should have done it. Anyone with any courage would have slammed down the receiver and run out of the hotel, meaning what they said. Why was she still holding it, still even listening? Because she always hoped to hear something she would never hear; to feel something she would never feel.

'Angela? Are you there?'

She sniffed furiously. 'Yes.'

'I've explained it badly. It isn't so difficult. We can easily find a doctor, I'm sure. It's only a question of—'

The two girls were getting up, clasping their little hand-bags. Tony was getting up, looking at his watch.

'All right. I'll ring you next week.'

'But you're coming home next week—you've got to see Fickstein on Friday—'

'That's what I mean. I'll ring you before I come home. Then if you haven't found anyone, I can stay here.'

'But—'

'I must go now. Sorry. Good-bye.'

She pushed the door open, hurried across the lounge. The two girls looked at her with prim, pink smiles.

'Do you know—?' Tony murmured.

'No. No, I don't think we do.' Her handbag was slung over her shoulder; her feet were enormous; her nails were dirty. She said to Tony, 'Did you get me a drink?'

'Annabel asked us to go along to this party—'

'Did you get me a drink?'

'No,' he said. 'I didn't.'

They looked at each other. The two girls rustled as they breathed, creaked, snapped like undergrowth.

'I'm tired,' Angela said. 'You go to the party.'

In the brief moment of hesitation she waited for a miracle.

'Are you sure?' he asked.

She nodded.

'You can tell me—you know, the news, tomorrow.'

She nodded again. Permission granted. Good-bye, Tony. Oh, please, make this stop happening.

'Well, then—' he said uneasily.

'Good-bye.' She gave them all exactly the same smile and felt herself turning, walking across the foyer, her hand pushing the revolving doors, the cold air. She hadn't brought her bicycle and she had no money. She began walking. I'll never get there, I'll never get there. And with each 'never' she stepped forward, so that she seemed to other people to be walking quickly, with determination, as though she might be late.

Chapter 23

RUTH SAT by the dead telephone with the feeling of someone who has been told to spin straw into gold. Slowly, hardly realising what she was doing, she eased off her shoes.

'Well,' Miss de Beer said, appearing in the doorway at the end of the passage. She started forward, her hands nervously twisting together. 'Well, perhaps I could have a word with you now, Mrs. Whiting?'

'Yes,' Ruth said wearily. 'I suppose so.'

'I have had the most terrible day, the most upsetting day.'

'I'm sorry.'

'Naturally, I telephoned Mr. Whiting. I had no idea where you had gone. Anything might have happened.' She was in tears. 'Going off like that without a word. It was a dreadful thing to do, Mrs. Whiting, dreadful.'

'I'm sorry,' Ruth said.

'Mr. Whiting is coming down on the 7.15. I insisted on it. I told him, I can no longer take the responsibility.'

'Tonight? But he said he couldn't—that he wouldn't be able to get back—'

'It is extremely inconvenient for him.'

'But I just wanted to do some shopping! I just wanted to—'

'You could have told me.'

'Miss de Beer, I'm thirty-seven years old, I've got three children, I'm used to living alone. I'm not used to telling someone every time I want to go out of the room!'

'Only a fortnight ago you were in a state of nervous collapse—'

'But you were all willing to send me off to France!'

'But you said you were not well enough to go!' Miss de Beer snapped triumphantly.

'Oh, all right—' What did it matter? 'I left the car at Ramsbridge. Perhaps you would tell Mr. Whiting when he arrives. And you'd better make the spare-room bed.'

'I have already done that. Might I ask how you got back from Ramsbridge without the car?'

'I walked.'

'You did *what?*'

'I came on a broomstick.'

'Mrs. Whiting!'

'Oh, I came back with Mr. Johnson, for heaven's sake.'

Lights through the fog had been receding moons, spinning into blackness; the distance between Ramsbridge and the Common had become, in her mind, an eternity of hills and valleys in which, in spite of Angela, in spite of Angela's child, she might die. Seeing Robert leaping along through the yellow mist she had asked him to bring her home.

'You weren't feeling well enough to drive,' Miss de Beer stated conclusively.

'Nonsense. The car wouldn't start. The battery's flat or something. Good-night, Miss de Beer.'

'But when Mr. Whiting arrives—?'

'Tell him I've gone to bed.'

She was not asleep when he arrived. He came unusually

quietly up the stairs; the door creaked open; she saw his big shape silhouetted against the landing light.

'Ruth?' His voice was almost gentle. 'Ruth? Are you awake?'

He tiptoed across the room and she felt him standing by the bed, looking down at her. She was puzzled. Why doesn't he switch on all the lights, get it over? But he just stood there. At last, when she felt she couldn't bear the steady, silent gaze a moment longer, he turned and crept heavily to the door. She opened her eyes but the door closed and she was alone.

'My dear child,' he said next morning, bathed, shaved and in his dressing-gown, sitting on the edge of her bed, 'I'm not blaming you. But why didn't you come and see me? We could have had lunch together.'

She couldn't believe it. 'Well, I didn't think—'

'You didn't even ring me, did you?' he asked, sadly reproving.

'No, I—'

'And you didn't ring the flat?'

'No.'

He lit a cigarette. She watched him uneasily. She had learned never to trust him, but he could still tempt her; still, by some rare gentleness, betray her into hope.

'Well, you put the wind up our Miss de Beer all right.'

She laughed carefully. 'Yes, I'm afraid so.'

'She insisted on my coming down. I had to scrap a couple of meetings.'

'I'm sorry. It wasn't a bit necessary.'

'Oh, well.' He patted her foot under the bedclothes. 'Of

course I'd much rather be here with you. I don't enjoy staying up in town at the weekends, you know that.'

'No, I'm sure you don't.'

'No. Well.' He got up, leaving her free to move. 'You left the car at the station, I hear.'

'Yes. It—it wouldn't start.'

'Tanner's going down to Ramsbridge this morning. I'll go down with him and pick it up. By the way, what's all this about some party of Rackworth's?'

'I don't know. What party?'

'I went round to the Tanners' last night when I found you were asleep. They were all jabbering about it. Some rock-and-roll party. Apparently all the village has been asked.'

'Oh . . . Oh, yes. I don't know where I put it.'

'Put what?'

'The invitation. We did have one. Look—on the mantelpiece.'

He read it frowning. 'Extraordinary thing,' he said. 'The man must be mad.'

'I'd forgotten all about it. When is it?' She tried to sound interested and overdid it. She sounded eager.

'Tonight. You don't want to go, do you?'

'Well, wouldn't you like to? I mean, it's so dull for you here—'

'Dull? Why should it be dull?'

'Well, you know—I thought—'

'Good God, you don't really want to spend the evening cavorting with a lot of farmers, do you? I certainly don't.'

'No,' she said. 'No, of course not.'

'Well, why do you think I would, then?'

So easily, without even noticing it, he had slipped back

into his natural, hectoring voice, his natural state of exasperation. She got quickly out of bed, pulled on her dressing-gown, went over to the chest of drawers.

'I suppose you didn't even answer the invitation, did you?'

Where he couldn't see her, standing with her hands resting on an open drawer, she closed her eyes for a moment. There was nothing behind them. She took out stockings, underclothes, pushed the drawer shut with her body.

'Is there another doctor round here?' she asked casually. 'I mean, apart from John.'

'What's that got to do with answering Rackworth's invitation?'

'Nothing. Why should it have?'

'What's the matter with John?'

'Nothing at all. I only—'

'You've taken against John now. Why?'

'I haven't, Rex, really—'

'Then why do you want to know?'

'Oh—' She turned away from him, clasping the few clothes tightly. It was a black morning, the last of November. Rain thrashed down on the evergreens, the bare trees were sodden. The butcher's boy, in black oilskin, came labouring up the drive on his bicycle. 'It doesn't matter,' she said. 'I was only interested.'

'There are plenty of doctors in Ramsbridge, I suppose.'

'Yes, I suppose there are.'

'But John's a very good doctor, as far as I know.'

'Oh, he is.'

'Everyone here goes to him, don't they?'

'Yes.'

'Well then why, for God's sake, do you want to know if there's anyone else?'

'I—' She was blinking, like someone who has been repeatedly struck. 'I only asked,' she said.

'But why,' patiently, 'did you ask?'

She ran, although it was such a short distance, to the bathroom; actually running, lifting her knees and feet, slamming and locking the door behind her. She sat down on the cork-topped stool and wrapped herself in her own arms, holding herself still, holding her breath. At last she heard him going downstairs and softened, drawing her fingertips down her cheeks and lodging them on her lips, the breath warming her cold fingers.

Chapter 24

A<small>T</small> BREAKFAST, they were husband and wife, sitting opposite each other with the two newspapers folded on their plates, the electric toaster generating toast, the electric percolator bubbling, the marmalade in a beehive jar. Ralph Rackworth's invitation lay on the table like a marker put down in a game of tug-o'-war. Although Rex had put it there, neither of them looked at it.

'When does Angela come home?'

'Next Thursday.'

'I hope she's not going to spend all the holidays mooning about as usual.'

Ruth smiled, poured the coffee.

'What about that boy? Does she say anything about him?'

'I think she sees him sometimes.'

'I must say I liked him. Did you like him?'

'Yes. Yes, he was all right.'

There was silence. Ruth looked at the invitation. Rock and Roll in Rackworth House! Mr. and Mrs. Rex Whiting are invited to meet their neighbours. No decorations, no swords.

'What about the boys?'

'The boys?'

'When do they get back?'

'Oh. On the 18th.'

'I suppose it's nearly Christmas.'

'Yes. It's December the first tomorrow.'

It was not so much a conversation as a furtive and isolated probing into the future. She did not notice his unusual interest in the arrival of the children. He did not notice that for once she knew what date it was. Normally she was the sort of woman who looks out of the window to discover, by what natural phenomena there may be, which season it is.

He pulled the invitation towards him, spinning it round on the polished table.

'Everyone's got one of these things, apparently.'

'I know.' Foolishly, she had not followed his change of mood. 'When Angela comes home—'

'The Tanners are going. So are the Johnsons.'

'Oh, they think they've got to, since the village has been asked. I expect everyone's going.' Absorbed in difficulty, she wandered without thinking into familiar dangers. Only later did she think whatever made me say that, I knew it was fatal.

He lit a cigarette, laying the spent match carefully on the edge of the plate, straightening it.

'In that case,' he said, 'I suppose it would look rather odd if we didn't turn up.'

'Why don't you go, then?'

'But you didn't answer the invitation, did you?'

'No, but you can ring up, you can explain.'

'I suppose you forgot?'

'I didn't think I'd be here.'

'But you didn't write and say you wouldn't be here?'

'No, Rex. No, I didn't. Oh, *please*—what does it matter?'

'I should have thought it was a question of common politeness.'

How can you, she thought, staring at him; how can you care so much? The flow of cruelty, which he called reason, would run, a thin, poisonous stream, into every hole and pocket of the day. There would be no time or place left to think in. Nothing, nothing would be allowed but this futile, meaningless problem of Rackworth's party. He wouldn't go without her. She should have realised that. You're a grandfather, she wanted to shout. Will you listen to the truth for once? You're a grandfather, not a little boy torturing flies! She clenched her fists against her forehead, beating herself down.

'Now,' he sighed weightily, 'what are you upset about?'

She had managed it. She got up, picking up the newspaper which she would never read.

'We'll go if you like,' she said.

He was cheated. 'But you don't want to go.'

'Yes, I would quite like to go.'

'Then why didn't you answer the invitation, like everyone else?'

She hesitated. The idea came to her that if she flattened her hands on either side of his head, holding it as though in a vice, he might be still. His persecution of her, of himself, was little more than a loud noise to fill an unbearable silence. She looked at his heavy, polished chins, his sharp nose thrusting out between eyes as dead as glass; the straight, already greying eyebrows.

'Do you feel lonely?' she asked.

'What?'

She was standing in the doorway, rubbing her cheek with the folded newspaper. 'Do you feel lonely, ever?'

'Yes,' he said, as though hypnotised. 'Sometimes.'

She nodded and went away, closing the door with a kind of reluctance. After a few moments he began to be upset.

Chapter 25

WHEN RALPH RACKWORTH'S father was a baby—looking much the same as he did now, and always suffering from croup—these rooms had often blazed for parties. Oh, the fires in the bedrooms, the hair and the corseting, violins sawing till dawn; truffles and champagne, no very nice people reeling under the chandeliers, to be sure, but memorable. So memorable that even to this day the old man, in his deepest sleep, sometimes clapped his hands to his ears and whimpered.

Ralph, stalking about in the half-dark with his fur collar turned up, had ordered the removal of all valuables. This, he explained, was not because he was afraid of breakages, but of thieves from the Common. A platform had been erected at the far end of the drawing-room, under the dark glower of Rackworth ancestors. Here, through the long, foggy afternoon, with the chandeliers coldly glistening on maids polishing parquet, lolled four young men in zipped sweaters and jeans, aimlessly plunking and drumming their instruments, dousing their cigarettes in Crown Derby cups of China tea, scratching the tufts of disordered hair which hung over their eyebrows. The maids did not understand them, either what they said or what they intended. They polished from the platform towards the double doors thirty yards away, giggling a little and glancing back occasionally over the crest of their hips to see what the young men were doing. Ralph walked among them in his boots, drinking whisky out of a silver hip-flask.

His own friends were already installed about the house. Most of them spent the day lying on the floor listening to early African folk music. Some stayed in bed. One, Jocelyn MacDermott, encountered the General in a long, foggy corridor.

'I met a ghost,' he said to Ralph. 'It looked poorly.'

'That was my father,' Ralph said. 'He isn't dead yet.'

They huddled into their collars, passing the flask, watching the preparations through narrowed eyes.

The guests were asked for half-past nine. By this time, food and drink, enough for an army, was ready in the main dining-room. The young men had taken off their sweaters and appeared in neat white shirts through which it was possible to see the modest line of their vests. Ralph had changed into a blue suit of the same design as his usual clothes and grimly brightened, like General Gordon, with a scarlet cummerbund. He and MacDermott leant against a pillar, brooding. A girl in a skirt like a mermaid's tail, except that it stopped short at her pale knees, hobbled across the floor and said, 'Oh, there you are, dear. I've been looking all over for yew.'

They didn't speak. She shivered slightly, holding her bare arms and humming to keep her spirits up.

The villagers came in a solid block, pushing in through the double doors with a slow arrogance, the men with their hands in their pockets, wheeling immediately to their natural protection of the wall, the girls in chapped, giggling groups of print and satin, their hair goffered, their lips a thin, unyielding crimson. The mothers, toppling on little shoes, looked for chairs. There were none. The fathers rubbed the horny backs of their necks.

Ralph and MacDermott slid, without speaking, into action. Formal, serious, bending as though on oiled hinges, their hands almost, but not quite, touching the women's arms, directing and listening, they dispersed the hard knot of the crowd, moved them towards the dining-room, watched them, with a kind of harsh gentleness, eat and drink. At exactly the right moment the friends moved in, slipping into their allotted positions, introducing themselves. The young men thrummed quietly in the empty drawing-room. It was as peaceful as the first, dawn movements of a battle.

Most of the Commoners, like the villagers, came together. For this terrible ordeal they had even gone so far as to share cars, the men sitting bulkily in front, the women rustling and nervous in the back, like children. Many of them had dined together, in groups of four, before setting out. As the foreign helps had been asked too, awkward situations arose out of the washing-up. The Wilmington-Smiths' Swede arrived before they did, regal on a bicycle. 'I left the drying,' Meg said humbly, meeting her in the Ladies' Cloakroom. 'The drying,' she growled huskily, 'is what I most dislike.'

They had fortified themselves with ones for the road. They were determined to succeed, whereas the villagers, regarding the whole thing as an entertainment, were completely indifferent, provided they weren't cheated. The women wore black and surrounded Ralph with the impatient lust of ravens, screeching at his dead, unusual body. They thought this polite, but he stepped away from them, leaving them disconcerted.

'A most curious man. Darling, what *is* this?'

'Scotch. I thought you were drinking Scotch.'

'So I was. Oh, dear, there's Watson. Hullo, Mr. Watson!' A brilliant smile, an almost naughty wave to the gardener. 'Actually, he looks rather dashing. Are we all here?'

'No, the Tanners aren't here yet.'

'And I don't see the Whitings.'

'They were coming together. It's not all as it should be, you know that.'

'You mean about Ruth?'

'*No*, my dear. I mean about *Rex*—'

Grave, relaxed as a man playing a fish, Ralph was dancing with the Watsons' frightened daughter.

Chapter 26

How's it going?' Jane whispered, as they put on their coats in Ruth's bedroom. 'Any progress?'

'I've got to find a doctor. To send her to a psychiatrist.'

'But won't Fickstein send her to a psychiatrist?'

'No. It's got to be an ordinary doctor.'

Their voices, breathy and muffled as conspirators, carried dreadful alarm.

'But it's absurd, if he's going to do it in the end—'

'I know.'

'She'll be beginning to show very soon.'

'I know. Can we ask Maxine again?'

Jane glanced at her. 'No,' she said, 'I shouldn't ask Maxine.'

'But she'd be bound to know—'

'I shouldn't ask her. Wait. We'll think of something. There must be thousands of doctors—'

'Yes, but who?'

'I've got a cousin, but he's up in Durham, damn it. Still, if all else fails. When's she coming home?'

'Thursday. I'm sure if I asked Maxine—'

'You don't want to get involved with Maxine. You know how those people are.'

Not knowing, thinking of Jane's changed attitude as yet another obstacle to be overcome, Ruth said nothing. Jane, unable to explain, looked miserable.

'What a divine thing,' she said loudly, brightly, holding up the musical box. 'What is it?'

'A musical box. You turn the handle—there, on the side.'

The tune spurted out, first fast, then slow. Nodding in time, smiling stupidly, Jane kept turning.

'It's "Bye Baby Bunting,"' she discovered eagerly. 'But how *sad!*

> *"Bye Baby Bunting,*
> *Daddy's gone a-hunting,*
> *Gone to fetch a rabbit skin—"'*

'I bought it for Lucinda,' Ruth said roughly. As no one ever used Baby's proper name, this was a surprise. 'But then I thought she was too young. So I kept it.'

'How wise. She smashes everything,' Jane said coldly.

The misunderstanding between them was, for the moment, complete. They went downstairs to Rex and Richard finishing the whisky.

'One for the road,' Rex demanded. He looked flushed and, in one of his London suits, uncomfortable.

'We're madly late,' Jane said. 'Ruthless Ralph will never forgive us.'

Rackworth House, as they came to it at the end of the long drive, threw off light like a liner in mid-ocean. The music could be heard outside but the people crossing and recrossing the bright, high windows seemed to move like ghosts.

'This is for Angela,' Richard Tanner said heartily. 'Why isn't Angela here?' He lurched a little going towards the front door and saluted a damp, crumbling statue. 'Come on in, old boy. Don't hang about. Nothing to be ashamed of.' Head down, he plunged in through the open doorway.

'Terrifying!' Jane hissed, taking one look. 'I do declare Ruthless Ralph is off with our Bessie. And can that be Lorna? My God,' she added soberly, 'it is.'

Ruth was in a dream, an absentee, noticing nothing. Her eyes, in the last weeks, had become great shadows in a face as small and wavering as a reflection in water. All the brisk, conscious movements of her body had been forgotten; she moved like a child, reluctantly, with grace, standing with her hands hanging at her sides or sitting as though this were the natural position for rest. She was wearing dead brown, the colour and texture of dried leaves; and this only because her black dress, the obvious, was now too big for her.

'You're as thin as Angela,' Rex had said with disgust. And she had said correctly, 'No. Thinner.' Angela now had weight to carry.

The young men had unbuttoned their shirts and were straddling the platform, braying and shuffling on bent, rigid legs like small boys who have gone too far. The lyrics, yelled by the youngest of them, were wordless.

> '*I e'er 'e 'ore I i-n-ng a Looos*
> *I e'er aw a I e'er ooze—*'

' "Your *love*, dear," ' sang Bessie happily, grinning up at the dedicated, expressionless face. ' "You got me singin' the blues—" '

' "Moon and stars—" ' howled young Watson in Meg Wilmington-Smith's ear, ' "No longer shine—" '

' "Lost the love—" ' Robert Johnson shouted recklessly, spinning Mary Budge like a bright penny, ' "I thought was mine—" '

> *'There's nothing left for me to do,*
> *But cry-ei-ei-ei over you—'*

'One moment,' MacDermott murmured. He didn't look at Ralph, but stood in the middle of the dance floor with his head down, looking at his suede boot, as though listening.

'Yes?'

'Who's that woman by the door?'

An impassive flicker. 'I haven't the faintest idea. Some bitch from the Common.'

MacDermott moved back to the pillar. He was drunk. He hadn't got Ralph's resistance to this sort of thing. He cracked up, releasing himself in solitary bouts of weeping, or even prayer. He was no good. He cut his hair like Ralph, wore the same sort of clothes, shrouded himself in mystery. But there wasn't anything to be mysterious about. Oh God, he thought, why aren't I vicious enough?

'Good evening,' a thick, bald man in a flowered waistcoat said. 'We have to introduce ourselves, I think. My name's Phillips.'

MacDermott growled.

'I'm the G.P. in these parts. I'm told you're a medico yourself.'

'Who,' MacDermott asked despairingly, 'told you that?'

'Pretty little thing over there.' MacDermott followed the jerk of the bald head and saw the girl in the mermaid skirt smiling vivaciously. A boy in an open-necked shirt, one of

Ralph's farm-hands, pulled her on to the floor. Immediately her face hardened, aged by twenty years.

'In practice?' Phillips asked casually.

'Yes.'

'Might I ask where?'

'You might, but you wouldn't know it.' He was only succeeding in being rude; the icy contempt, the stony monosyllables were missing.

'I know most places,' Phillips wheedled patiently.

'Good for you,' MacDermott said. He pushed himself off the pillar and slouched away. He pushed through the doorway, looking hard at the woman in the brown dress. Her eyes passed over him without seeing. He half filled a glass with whisky, drank it and came back to her.

'Will you dance?'

Her mouth opened another darkness in her face.

'Come on,' he said roughly, and grabbed her wrist. When Ralph sees this, he thought obscurely, he'll be sorry.

Chapter 27

THEY DIDN'T SPEAK, walking round the floor in a remote embrace.

At last he asked, sourly, 'Do you live round here?'

'Yes.' They turned the corner and stepped resolutely on. 'Do you?' She knew, of course, that he didn't.

'No.'

She saw John Phillips standing by the pillar. He inclined his head and moved away. Avoiding me, she thought, hating him. Turned again, she saw his squat back pushing away through the crowd. She could feel him thinking there's the wretched mother having a good time while the poor child suffers. Anger began to make her lively. MacDermott felt the change in her and loosened his hold.

'It's going very well,' he said.

'Yes.' She was shocked to see Betty Johnson clinging to a young man whose staggering steps and white, glistening face showed that this was the first time he was going to be sick from drink. 'A terrific success,' she said. Betty Johnson opened her eyes and looked at her coldly; then her eyelids sank again and she rocked from foot to foot in the young man's arms.

'But do you think,' Ruth asked, 'we could stop dancing?'

'Certainly,' he said indifferently. 'What do you want, a walk in the conservatory?'

'No.'

'Let's have another drink.'

Lightly holding her hand, he led her through to the dining-room. Rex and Richard Tanner had made themselves comfortable round the enormous fireplace. The food was all gone, but there was still plenty to drink. An old man was snoring peacefully on an upright chair. MacDermott poured whisky into two used glasses.

'Well?'

She was standing with her back to Rex, holding her glass with both hands. 'What—what did you say?'

'Are you enjoying this democratic orgy?' He winced as he said it.

'Yes. Thank you.'

Her eyes flickered up, noticing him. She pretended to drink, but only let the warm, brackish whisky touch her lips.

'What's the mystery?' Sadly, he listened to himself.

'What do you mean?' she asked gently.

'What do you look so sad about?'

'Oh—' She knew now that Rex had seen her; she could feel him drilling into her back.

'What do you do?' she asked quickly. 'Are you a writer or something?'

'No.'

'What do you do, then?'

'See that pompous fool just coming through the door?'

She raised her eyes and saw John Phillips. He walked past without a sign of recognition. He would have joined the men by the fireplace.

'Yes.'

'Do you know him?'

'Yes.'

'Then let's go.' He took an unopened bottle and, again firmly, her hand.

'Where?' She hurried behind him without daring to look back. He didn't answer.

'Where are we going?' she insisted.

'Oh, come on.'

Halfway up the stairs he dropped her hand. 'You needn't come if you don't want to,' he said sulkily. 'You go back if you want to.'

Ruth looked down into the stone-flagged hall. Mary Budge came in through the open front door. She looked round, grasped her suspender belt firmly through her print dress and pulled it down over her hips. Then she patted her hair and walked off towards the dining-room.

'Why don't you like John Phillips?'

'I loathe doctors. You'd better go back, I suppose.'

Robert Johnson came in through the front door. He looked round, smoothed his hair with two cupped hands and hurried into the cloakroom labelled Men. Ruth clung with one hand to the banisters.

'Why?'

'For the same reason I hate Freemasons, Rotarians, Trades Unions, Boy Scouts. If I do the same job, it doesn't give that rubber-faced fool the right to clap me on the back—I'm told you're a medico yourself, old boy, old boy. Christ.' He climbed on, full of disgust, towards the dim landings.

At the top he turned, looking down over his shoulder.

'You're not coming, I suppose. Good-night, then.'

She followed him, at first almost running, down the long

corridor. He did not look back, but held the green baize door open for her, then plodded on up more stairs, through more doors, so that she felt as she had at Fickstein's, as though she were being led through fortifications.

'This is Ralph's flat,' he said. 'Have you been here before?'

She shook her head. In the room where no piece of furniture was more than eighteen inches high, and where there was very little furniture anyway, he seemed enormously tall. Even she felt awkward, heron-like, having to bend to everything.

'Sit down. I'll get some glasses.'

She crouched on the floor, among cushions. Because there was no fireplace, it seemed cold; yet as they had come into the flat the air had been warm as a greenhouse.

'It's a beautiful room,' she said, shivering.

'You think so?' The music beat far beneath them, a subterranean din. MacDermott squatted opposite, cross-legged, arranging the glasses, the whisky, the soda on a black marble slab. He was now extremely nervous, regretted having come. He continually looked towards the door as though expecting an urgent summons to be answered.

'We'll have a quick one,' he said. 'Then go back. Ralph's put a lot into this. He's a remarkable man. Do you know him at all?"

'No, I hardly know him at all. We don't—'

'Some people think he's a fool to live here, but it suits his mentality, it gives him freedom, you understand me? Of course not everyone has the courage to live the way they want, even given the money. An excess of courage is the same thing as madness, if you get my meaning.' He looked hopelessly away from her. 'But naturally you don't.'

She looked down into her glass. 'Are you,' she asked, 'a doctor?'

'Ralph lives in a fantasy all right. Look at this room. You say it's beautiful. I say it's an excess of courage added to an excess of wealth. It's not comfortable. It's not fashionable. He has a deep freeze. He likes the noise. What does he keep in it? One packet of peas and a Christmas pudding left over from last year. You only get excess like that in dreams. Am I right?'

'What's your name?' she asked.

'Names? What are names? I haven't asked you yours. I don't want to know it. You know what would happen if I knew your name? We'd discover that my great uncle met your mother at a church bazaar in Upper Norwood in 1931.'

She was startled. 'Would we? But I'm sure my mother didn't—'

'All right.' He got up, finishing his drink. 'Let's go.'

She took a deep breath. 'I prefer it here.'

'Why?' he asked dismally.

'I—I just do. Can I have another drink?'

'You haven't finished that one.'

She finished it, unable to prevent a grimace of disgust, and held out her glass.

'You don't like it,' he said gently.

'Yes, I do.'

'You're married, I suppose.' He looked at her for the first time, weighing up the smudge of brown, the shadowed eyes, the nervous hands. 'Happily, I hope. Or are you suffering?'

'What—'

'What do I mean?' He sighed, lay down on the floor, propped on his elbow. 'Oh, you're suffering for some reason.

Your husband's a brute. Your lover's left you. Your little world is plunged in darkness. You're a poor little woman who thinks that by coming up here with me something, God knows what, but something, is going to be solved. Am I right?'

'Yes. I mean I didn't think—'

'Oh, for God's sake. I don't solve anything. Why not pick on one of those beefy labourers? Ralph would probably recommend one. I'll ask him if you like. Guaranteed genuine muscle throughout. I doubt whether you'd even be bothered with blackmail.'

'You're very silly,' she said, primly, kneeling, her hands pressed together in her lap.

'I'm what?'

'Ridiculous.'

'I am.' He grinned suddenly. 'What's your problem?'

'Well—'

But she found that she didn't want to tell him. She had never been further from her life than she was now— anonymous, a woman he had picked out for whatever reason; a mystery. She could tell him she was a widow, an adored demi-mondaine, a pottery maker from Bath. She could have a great love, her own; a storm of which she was the sad, mysterious centre. Why spoil it all? She got up and walked softly across the room, disappearing into the shadows, her dress rustling like grass. 'It's a little difficult,' she said, from a distance.

'Of course.'

'Are you really a doctor?'

He hesitated, groaned slightly. 'Yes. I don't do abortions, if that's what you want.'

There was a long pause. 'But you are a doctor?'

'Good God, I've told you. I work in a bin.'

'In a bin?'

'A lunatic asylum. A madhouse.'

'You mean with mad people?'

'That's right.'

'Oh.'

There was another long silence. The music vibrated now with the frenzy of a pneumatic drill; the heavily shrouded windows shook.

'What are you doing over there, anyway?'

'Nothing.'

'Why don't you come and sit down? You make me nervous, wandering about.'

Reluctantly, she came back and settled on the cushions, her skirt spreading and subsiding like wings. He swivelled round, propping his head on her knees.

'Since we're staying,' he said morosely. She looked down at him with alarm as though he had said, of his head, 'Just hold this for a minute, will you?'

UNDRESSING, AT HOME, at three in the morning, Ruth moved as quickly and absently as though she were alone; even, cleaning her face, unfolding her night-gown, humming to herself. She was not deliberately over-looking Rex, who sat on the stool at the foot of the bed looking, as though contemplating the effort, at his shoes. It was just that for once he was silent. His presence was identified by noise.

He waited, increasingly anxious. She got into bed, lay down, switched off the light on her side of the bed, turned over, sighed deeply and was still. He was left in the half-dark with the realisation that if he wanted to sit all night on the stool staring at his shoes, he could.

'Ruth?' He had to repeat it more loudly. 'Ruth?'

A querying noise, no more.

He waited a few moments until her breathing had become even and deep. 'Are you asleep?'

She scuffled on the mattress as though trying to get inside it. His discomfort could not wait. He got up and walked, tensed with his hands in his pockets, to the side of the bed.

'Ruth!'

She recognised through her light, warm sleep that he

was there. A tremendous reluctance made her pretend to go on sleeping.

'I don't want to quarrel with you,' he mumbled. 'I must talk to you.'

She was wide awake. There was something new in his voice. It's only a trick, she told herself. Nevertheless, she opened her eyes, blinking up at him.

'Won't it do in the morning?'

'No. I shan't be able to sleep.'

'Oh. I see.'

He began to walk up and down. The knowledge that MacDermott would see Angela on Thursday was like someone holding her hand in reassurance under the bedclothes. He had turned out to be an ordinary man: ordinarily helpful, ordinarily kind, glad to do what she asked, but relieved that she asked so little. 'We'll fix it. Sleep well, grandma.' She hadn't liked that at the time. Now, faced with Rex in labour with his emotions, it was a comfort.

'Sometimes,' he said, 'you seem to think I have no feelings.'

'I'm sorry.'

'I suppose you were paying me back.' He stopped, turned to her with an extraordinary urgency. 'Were you?'

'What do you mean?' she asked, bewildered.

'What were you doing all that time?'

'All what time?'

'This evening, for Christ's sake! An hour and a half! I suppose you'll tell me you were playing cat's cradle. What? What were you doing?' His voice was shaking, but not entirely with anger. It seemed to burst out of the wrong part of him, as though clumsily forced. His big, portly body looked absurdly crumpled; in his distress he had pushed his fingers through his hair which stood up thinly, showing the pink scalp beneath.

She sat up a little. 'I was talking,' she said wonderingly.

'You? Talking?' He laughed theatrically, then pounced. 'What about?'

'I don't know.'

'If you were talking for an hour and a half you must know what you were talking about. What?'

'I said I don't remember. This man was a friend of Ralph's, of Rackworth's. We talked about him, and about the party, and—'

'Where did you go? No one knew where you were.'

'We went up to Ralph's flat.'

'Was anyone else there?'

'No, but—'

'So you talked for an hour and a half in Rackworth's flat. Alone. While my friends downstairs—'

'Oh, Rex, don't be absurd! I was talking. I was just talking.'

'You went to bed with that crew-cut spiv,' he said, 'didn't you?'

'No.'

'Then what were you doing? What on earth were you doing all that time?'

'I've told you,' she said. Their voices chorused. 'Just talking.'

'I don't believe you.'

'Why don't you believe me? Because it's not what you would have done?'

His face was haggard at the foot of the bed. 'All right,' he said. 'Out with it. Now we get the sense of the thing.

Let's get it over, for God's sake. It's not what I would have done.'

'I'm sorry,' she said quietly. In one movement she slipped down into the bed again. 'Let's go to sleep. It's so late. I'm sorry.'

He was silent for so long that she almost began to sleep again. When she heard the relentless 'Ruth,' it came from very near, was almost gentle. She again opened her eyes. He was kneeling by the bed, his face only a few inches away. It's really true, she thought. He's really feeling something. She was confused; unable, after so long, to understand. She knew he was uncomfortable crouching there.

'Please tell me.'

'Tell you what?' She had almost forgotten Angela herself. What did he want, so badly, to know? 'Tell you what?' she repeated desperately.

'I know,' he said, with great difficulty, 'that it's all been wrong with us. You think I've behaved badly. I have behaved badly. I'm a natural bastard, that's my trouble.'

Her one exposed eye became alert, wary. Could he be trying to charm her again? She looked for signs, the upper lip stiffened, as though by feeling, the boyish droop of eyelids, the stout, middle-aged face deprecating and humble and pathetic. But he looked at her simply, frowning a little.

'You asked me this morning if I felt lonely. Well, I do.'

'Yes,' she said, concentrating.

'You don't have to be pleasant to be lonely, you know. In fact, the more unpleasant you are, the more you feel it.'

She nodded in the pillow, her eye still fixed, guarded.

'And then what you do, to get out of it I mean, is more unpleasant than anything else. Which doesn't mean that you don't know it is. Understand?'

'No.'

He sighed. He was too heavy to be on the floor, and cramped. He pulled himself up and sat on the side of the bed. She moved her legs away, giving him room.

'About this MacDermott,' he said. 'I don't blame you. I blame myself. I don't want you to think I blame you, that's all.'

'Because,' she asked, hardly knowing what she meant, but knowing him so well, 'that makes you feel better?'

'I suppose so. You're still young. You looked damned attractive tonight. I don't blame you.'

He had forgiven her and this forgiveness, she knew, was deeply important. It gave him confidence, bridged the emptiness between them, comforted him for whatever crimes he thought he had committed. To be able to forgive her for one act which he could understand, but of which she was unfortunately innocent, could bring them both some peace. She understood this. It was too late, but she understood it.

'The fact is,' he said heavily, 'I'm very fond of you.'

She kept her voice gentle. 'Because of tonight?'

'I realised it tonight,' he said rather pompously. Then, pouncing again, 'You admit it then? I'm right? You did let that swine make love to you? What?'

She couldn't help smiling. It was irreverent as a smile in church, at a funeral, an uncontrollable warmth melting a face of pious stone. As an admission of guilt, she realised, as she turned into the pillow, it was more than enough.

'All right.' He got up, his voice dull. 'I've told you. I don't blame you.'

'But—'

'I won't even say you might have picked more suitable

surroundings. Or thought of the children. Particularly Angela. Of course I don't expect you to think of me.'

'But Rex—'

'I understand why you did it.' His forgiveness was protracted, might even go on for years. 'We won't mention it again.'

'Good,' she breathed, lying down.

He began to undress. From time to time he thought of something else to say and halted, his tie half undone, one leg freed from his trousers, his vest hanging from one arm; but always thought better of it and moved on. Finally he got into bed and turned out his light. They lay in the darkness, waiting.

At last he moved, his hand groping for her.

'We could start again,' he said. 'After this.'

Horror, unwelcome, almost bitterly resented, petrified her.

'No.'

His hand stiffened.

'Not now,' she said into the pillow. 'Please.'

His hand dropped, withdrew quickly. 'All right,' he said. 'I understand.' His sensibility filled him with awe, with respect for himself. 'Maybe, though, later.'

She nodded in the darkness. But the horror stayed. She slept with it, murmuring, twisting, crying out, until morning.

Chapter 29

UT WHY,' Angela asked, 'do I have to go alone? All that way, and it's pitch dark.'

'It's hardly any way at all. Your bicycle lamp works, I tried it.'

'What about coming back? I'll have to push it up that hill. Honestly.'

This time there had been no feverish welcome when the holidays began, no treats for tea or flowers in the bedroom. Angela had arrived with her books, her small canvas grip, wearing a skirt and black woollen stockings. The skirt was done up with a safety-pin, the gaping placket covered with a long, darned, medical student's sweater. She had pulled her hair back into a thick rubber band and her face was pinched, sunken with cold.

'Besides,' she said, 'I feel dreadfully sick.'

'Then I'll drive you,' Ruth said uneasily. But I won't come in. You understand?'

'The whole thing seems so stupid. Sneaking about in the middle of the night, Rackworth House of all places. Couldn't you have found a proper doctor?'

'He is a proper doctor.'

'Well, I don't know. It seems awfully stupid.'

She flung herself into an armchair, her legs askew, and began to look at *Vogue*. All emotions, regret, fear, loneliness, seemed to have resolved themselves in bad temper. She was angry with everyone, and didn't know why. With her mother most of all. If I were married, she thought bitterly, she'd be knitting. She didn't want to be married, or to have a child to knit for. It was just, obscurely, the principle of the thing. A person needs looking after and they send you out on bicycles, in the dark, in the fog. What a welcome.

'I thought we might do some shopping tomorrow,' Ruth said energetically. 'After we've seen Fickstein.'

'Oh God, not all that Oxford Street, please.'

'We'll just go to Harrods. I want to get some boxing gloves for Julian.'

'I bet you can't get boxing gloves in Harrods.'

'Oh, I expect you can.' It was like pushing a heavy weight up a hill, chattering all the time. 'What would you like for Christmas?'

'I don't know. Nothing.'

'I thought you might like a dress. You know, for parties. A pretty one.' She felt as though she was describing a shroud.

'What on earth for? I don't wear dresses at parties.'

'What do you wear, then?'

'Oh, I don't know—' She went back to glowering at the mink and leather.

In a few weeks, Ruth thought, trying not to look at her, she will be different. If she were married, we might be sitting here talking about the baby. We should have something to talk about. A boy or a girl, and what about names? You don't have to worry, it's not nearly as bad as they make out and anyway you forget. You forget this, too. Well, you'll need at least three dozen and I suppose in the nursing home they'll want them marked. I'll mark them for you. Don't lift things, you're certainly not going to ride that bicycle, I'll drive you. I might even be knitting. Both knitting, two women on either side of the fire, yawning and talking, waiting for the months to crawl by.

Instead of this, there would be nothing.

'How's Tony?'

'He's all right.'

'Do you still see him?'

'Oh, for heaven's sake, what is this? The Inquisition or something? I see him sometimes. Of course I do.'

Miss de Beer came in with the supper on a tray. It was stew, the lumps of meat and carrot swimming in pale, greasy liquid. There was no room on the coffee table for everything, the stew and the plates, the dish of collapsed potatoes, the dish of mashed and weeping sprouts.

'So cosy,' she said. 'Supper by the fire.'

Angela looked at the food with loathing and hunched herself behind the magazine.

'Mrs. Whiting must be glad to have you back. Aren't you, Mrs. Whiting?'

'Of course,' Ruth said, smiling brightly.

'A daughter must be such company. My own mother was my best friend. Never a secret that wasn't shared. She was a great loss to me.'

'She must have been,' Ruth said.

'Will you have coffee after?' Coffee, she always implied, should be had with.

'No, thank you. We have to go out.'

'Out?'

'Yes.'

'In this fog?'

'Yes.'

There was a moment's hesitation. Miss de Beer's wits were at work. 'And if Mr. Whiting 'phones, can I tell him where to reach you?'

'We'll be back by ten.'

'Very well. I'll wait up.'

'Please don't bother.'

'If you are going out in this fog, at this time of night, Mrs. Whiting, the least I can do is to wait up. Mr. Whiting expects it of me.'

She stalked out, leaving a grimy oven-cloth on the tray among the congealing dishes.

'Why is that ghastly woman still here? Why can't we have supper in the kitchen, like we always do? Why don't we just have an egg or something?'

'I don't know!' Ruth wanted to shout. 'For heaven's sake, child, I don't know!' Instead, crouching, spooning out the repellent food, she said, 'Where will you have it? On your knee?'

'The mere sight of it makes me feel ill.'

Alone, silent, Ruth struggled through the meal. She felt awkward, as though she were doing something disgusting. Angela leafed through another, older *Vogue*. From time to time she sighed and heaved restlessly in the chair.

Ruth parked the car in the drive, switched off the engine. Leaves dripped and fog lapped against the windows. The bulk of Rackworth House was invisible. There was silence in the car except for a desolate and protracted sniff from Angela.

'Just ring the bell,' Ruth said uneasily, 'and say you've come to see Dr. MacDermott.'

'Supposing nobody answers?'

'Of course somebody will answer.'

'But they'll think it's so odd if I go alone. I don't know the man. I don't know the Rackworths. If you came, it'd be all right.'

This was reasonable. 'I can't explain,' Ruth said.

'Well, hell, it's come to something when *you* can't explain things.' She was crying, ferreting in the foggy dark for a handkerchief.

'You've got do *some* of this by yourself,' Ruth said deperately.

'I'll go and see Fickstein by myself tomorrow. Honestly I will. You can do your shopping or something. Please.'

'All right.' She had to give in.

'Not if you don't want to.'

'Of course I don't mind. Come on.'

The door was opened by a small, trembling old man in a green baize apron.

'Carol singers?' he enquired, peering cautiously.

'No, we came to see Mr. Rackworth,' Ruth said. 'But perhaps there's another door—'

'No, no. Come in. I was just—' he tried for a moment to remember, then, triumphantly, got it—'cleaning the silver. Nasty, cold job. You can't get servants to do it these days.'

The hall echoed, the double doors were closed. He began to climb the stairs with the determination of an ant creeping up a rock face.

'Very fortunate,' he said, 'that I was—cleaning the silver. That is why I heard the bell. On a Wednesday or Friday, for instance, I would not have heard the bell. Ralph's friends, of course, use the side entrance.'

'I'm sorry,' Ruth said. 'I didn't know.'

'Perfectly all right. As it happened, I heard the bell. Did you come to the ball last week?'

'The ball?'

'Ralph, my son, had a ball, you know. Perfectly dreadful noise. Worse, I think,' he stopped, his hand trembling on a doorknob, considering, 'I think considerably worse than in my mother's day. Yes. Worse. Considerably worse.'

'Oh dear,' Ruth said.

'My wife didn't hear it, of course. She is slightly deaf.'

'I'm sorry,' Ruth said, glancing at Angela, wishing she would say something, 'to bring you all this way.'

'Not in the least. I thought it was early for carol singers. But they make no effort, you know. Just ring the bell. Without singing. So you never know. Men with goods from the blind, too, hairbrushes and so on. One's always to and fro.'

'It must be difficult.'

'There's little else to do. Clean the silver. Answer the bell. Play a game of dominoes from time to time. Dust the begonias.'

'What?'

'A little pruning. We live quietly and, fortunately, no wireless. You are from London I take it?'

'No. No, we live on the Common.'

'Ah, yes.' He tried, but couldn't place it. He looked gently at Angela. 'And is your mother well?'

'This is my mother,' Angela said, alarmed.

'Of course. Foolish of me.' He paused outside the door of Ralph's flat. 'What name shall I say?'

'It doesn't matter,' Ruth said quickly. 'Thank you so much.'

'Excuse me.' He opened the door, then hesitated, forgetting. 'What name shall I say?'

'Whiting,' Angela numbled. 'Mrs. and Miss Whiting,' she repeated clearly.

'Delighted to have met you.' He held out a skinny little hand, blackened with silver polish. 'Perhaps you will drop in one day for tea. In the spring.'

He hurried off down the corridor.

'Who on earth was that?' Angela gasped.

'I suppose it's General Rackworth.'

'But he's mad!'

'I'm sorry,' Ruth said, 'I mean, if he upset you.'

'I just don't see why it has to be like this, that's all. Mad generals. Your crazy friends. Not explaining things. This ghastly morgue.'

'You would have preferred the old woman in Cowley?'

They looked at each other in shocked silence. They were fighting over a dead child, in bitterness.

'Let's go in,' Angela snapped. 'Since we're here.'

She led the way, Ruth following.

Chapter 30

H E'S NICE,' Angela said.

'Yes.'

'They're both nice.'

'I'm glad you liked them.'

'I suppose they're queer as coots.'

'I don't know.' She nosed the car into the lane, through the fog. 'What is a coot, anyway?'

'I don't know. A kind of bird.'

'I thought it was a rabbit.'

'No, that's a coon. I don't know. Anyway, it's a good thing you met him—at the ball.'

They both laughed briefly.

'Anyway,' Ruth said, 'it's the first step over.'

'Yes.'

Miss de Beer met them as they came, shivering and yawning, through the back door.

'Mr. Whiting 'phoned,' she said, with satisfaction. 'And Mrs. Tanner 'phoned. She wants you to ring her back.'

'Thank you.'

Miss de Beer's eyes were busy on Angela, the unstamped, but addressed envelope she was clutching.

'Did you want a stamp?' she asked. 'I have plenty. I can give it to the postman in the morning.'

'No, thank you.'

'It's no trouble.'

Angela stuffed the letter into her pocket and pushed out of the kitchen.

'We shall be going up to town tomorrow,' Ruth said. 'On the 8.10. We'll get our own breakfast.' Explaining everything she was going to do was more exhausting than doing it. She waited for the inevitable, 'To town? Tomorrow?' and nodded dumbly.

'I hope you will let Mr. Whiting know?'

Ruth mumbled good-night and went to the telephone. I must get rid of her, she thought. I can't bear it. She'll find out. I know she will.

'Jane?'

'Ruth. You were out.' The voice was deeply accusing.

'I'm sorry.' She was not going to explain any more. 'Did you want me?'

'Have you heard about Robert? I suppose if you've been out you must have. Isn't it *terrifying*?'

Ruth sat down. Unreasonably, strongly, she didn't want to hear about Robert. She was tired. She didn't want to hear. She gathered up her disbelief like a small, inadequate covering.

'No,' she said. 'What is it?'

'My dear, he's in *hospital!*'

'Ill?'

'A fractured skull. It was Betty, apparently she nearly killed him, can you *imagine*?'

'Oh, no,' Ruth said. She shut her eyes. There was emptiness. 'It's not true.'

'But it is. He came home this evening, walked through the front door and wham. She did it with a clock. Just like that, not a word spoken. Then she 'phoned John and when he got there—'

'How do you know all this?'

'John stopped by for a drink on his way back from the hospital. She told him everything.'

'And he told you,' Ruth said dully.

'He was frightfully upset, I've never seen him so jumpy. I mean, after all, we're all friends. Heaven knows, none of us have got any secrets. Better to know facts, I would have thought, than just gossip.' She was prim, snappy.

Has he told them about Angela? Has Jane?

'And Betty?' she asked. 'How is she?'

'Fine. Packed his bag for the hospital, never said she was sorry or anything. Meg says there were strange goings-on at the Rackworth party and that started it all, though everyone knows Betty's insanely jealous anyway. I was too busy keeping Rex from breaking the place up to notice.'

'Well, you know about that.'

'Yes, *I* know. But no one else does. I must say you're getting the most lurid reputation, and of course one can't possibly explain about Angela and all. They're even saying that you and Robert—'

'Perhaps,' Ruth broke in harshly, "it would be better if we did explain.'

'About Angela? But you couldn't! You'd have to drag in Maxine and all that!'

'Maxine? Why?' Maxine seemed the least of it, an impression of a silly, pleasant girl, almost forgotten.

'Well, I mean . . . Oh, well, but you couldn't! What about Rex? What about Angela, come to that? You'd be crazy!'

'I know. Poor Robert.'

'I must say, it's quite a thing. First your little drama and now Robert hit over the head with a clock, and that *orgy* on Saturday, I don't know what we're all coming to. Was that young man helpful?'

'Yes. He wrote down a lot of lies.'

'Well, after all, it doesn't matter if they're lies. Is anything wrong?'

'Of course not.' She made a great effort to reach safer ground. 'How's Baby?'

'Oh, monstrous, as usual—' It was a success. The world might split like a cracked apple, death be expected, prepared for. Moons might ride the sky and love, doomed, struggle to grow in impossible places. Baby would still lisp the cute remark, refuse spinach, need unobtainable gaiters. Listening, Ruth felt drawn into a cult, a society, in which adult people were no longer required to stand alone, but were supported by their children. How can we move, think, breathe, they groaned, when impeded by these living crutches? But without them, life would be too dangerous; an emptiness in which, the most fearful thing of all, there would be no time, no landmarks.

'. . . And of course there she was at seven, demanding Mrs. Tiggy-winkle, so after two hours' sleep I was dead by nine—'

'I should think so,' Ruth said. She was thinking of the Johnsons, alone except for their hysterical dog. A dog was no use. The dog had probably seen the whole thing, sitting there scratching itself.

'You don't know how lucky you are,' Jane chattered, without meaning it, 'that yours are almost grown up. And then, even when Mike was a baby, you were so young. I'm just too old to be playing shopping at two in the morning, my heart isn't in it.'

'Then why do you?'

'My dear, one can't *refuse!*'

So it went on. There was no point at which it could stop. Baby had smoothed over all difficulties, reduced all problems to a digestible blob of junket in the bottom of an unbreakable, protecting bowl. Angela climbed into her pyjamas upstairs, not looking at herself in the mirror. Miss de Beer prayed to be diverted from temptation. Ralph Rackworth took MacDermott's queen and asked, as he did every night, 'You really want to go on with this?' All over the Common, women who were not telephoning felt more than usually frightened, crept in to watch television with their Mother's Helps, wrote to their children (*'Only another twelve days! Isn't it exciting?'*), made lists for Christmas. Visions of bicycles, air-guns, chemistry sets floated across their anxious minds, miraculously calming. We, they told themselves, are all right, safe; nothing can ever happen to us. They longed for their husbands and, in the uneasy night, almost fell in love again.

Ruth sat for a long time in her bedroom. The Johnsons and Angela's child were confused in her mind, the senseless destruction of something loved, needed too much. But it was not Angela who loved the child. Who could love it, an embryo, blind, its seaweed limbs not even moving? It's not mine, she repeated to herself, it's not mine. And if she had really killed him, even if she intended to do it, there wouldn't have been anything left for her. She could never have put him back. Never. It would have been done for good; Robert, that particular gentle, goaded man, gone forever. The act of killing must be so easy—she thought of twigs snapped between the fingers, a mere handful of litter thrown away—but afterwards, surely, it must go on forever, a perpetual emptiness. Murder is irrevocable. To take it upon yourself is to assume that you are God, capable of granting immortality. But, she told herself desperately, it's not mine. I'm not doing it. It's not mine. No one is God, and death is the end of everything. But we must be practical; face facts; not, whatever happens, be sentimental. Robert is not an unborn child. He has lived longer.

There was no coherence in her thoughts; they mounted, uncontrolled, into a terrifying perception of violence. Long after Angela was asleep, curled and insensible as her child, Ruth struggled through a waking dream in which Mac-Dermott, Fickstein, the Johnsons, indulged themselves in death, telling her to join them, that this was reason.

Chapter 31

IN THE TRAIN the next morning she sat opposite Angela and was conscious of Robert in hospital, that one man was missing and probably missed by no one except herself. It seemed unjust that no one waited for him, looked for him, asked, 'Where's Johnson?' He must, she thought, have travelled on this train five days a week for over five years, except for the month that he and Betty dangerously ventured Portofino.

'Jackson's got 'flu,' the haggard man in the corner said, lowering his *Financial Times*, making a pronouncement.

'Got a touch of it myself,' the big man mumbled through his yellow moustache, shuddering. He had a large box of paper handkerchiefs balanced on his knee and pulled them out in handfuls, one handful to blow his nose, the next to clean up his moustache; then he would let down the window and send them flying, settling back with his eyes closed until, tortured, he pulled out the next handful.

'You should be in bed,' the haggard man said with sympathy.

'I'm in the middle of a case, tenth day, damned tricky. All very well for chaps like Jackson.' He sneezed violently. 'No good at the bar,' he gasped. He was very ill.

Do they mean Jackson, Ruth wondered, or Johnson? Do they know that Johnson has been killed, almost killed, by his wife? She longed to tell them.

Angela leant forward, whispered urgently, 'Do you think we could have the window open?' She was probably going to be sick. Ruth lowered the window a few inches and Angela stood up, breathing in fog and steam with her mouth open. The two men glared, hostile, at Ruth. She gave them a meaningless smile and looked away from them, energetically clearing a small space in the misted window and staring through it with fixed, mild interest.

My daughter is pregnant, she might say, and therefore feels sick, particularly when you sneeze. At last Angela sat down. She was clearly suffering.

'I think I'd better come with you,' Ruth said in a low voice.

Angela shook her head, her hands pressing down in her lap.

'I think I'd better.'

What she felt to be lack of sympathy had now turned, in Angela, to a bitter satisfaction. It was impossible to articulate what she felt: nobody loves me, nobody cares, I might as well be dead, I'm dragged about in dreadful trains, want a hot-water bottle, want cocoa, want treats and loving, they'll be sorry when I'm dead but if that's the way they want it I'll show them, nobody cares what I'm going through and they'll be sorry . . . and so on, a fathomless despair.

Nobody, she repeated hopelessly to herself, minds if I live or die. She didn't care about her child, her career.

Angela only cares about herself, Ruth thought. But being outside, a stranger, she interpreted this not as a need, but as an imperfection.

'You've got the letter?' she asked.

Angela nodded.

'You won't—' Ruth glanced at the two men, hesitated. 'Don't let him think you're—' She gave up, sitting back in her seat. Don't be indifferent, she had wanted to say. Don't just sit there as though you don't care. But she couldn't say it. 'Ask him how soon it will be. I mean, if you have to be away at Christmas.'

'But I can't be away at Christmas,' Angela muttered. She was deprived now of the heart of the year, even Christmas taken away from her, no stocking, no tree, no presents, no sixpence in the pudding; banished, alone. That they would allow this, even contemplate it, seemed the final treachery.

'But if they can't find a—' Again Ruth glanced at the two men. The one with the moustache was asleep, his heavy face jolting with the train; the other one was writing in a small black book. 'If they can't find a place before then—'

'I'll go after.'

'You can't, I told you, he's going away.'

'Then why don't we find someone else, for heaven's sake?'

The ill man woke up with a start; the haggard one put his book into his brief-case and placed his bowler hat carefully on his head.

'We can't find anyone else now,' Ruth said. 'You know we can't.'

Angela shrugged her shoulders. For the first time, she realised that she could refuse to have this done. She wasn't going to, of course, but she could. Then where would they all be?

'Anyway,' she said stiffly, 'I'll go alone, if you don't mind. I shall find it much easier, actually.'

The haggard man suddenly leant forward. He had a

186

kind, ravaged smile. His face, in the gloom of the carriage, glowed with an unhealthy irridescence.

'Excuse me,' he said, 'but I couldn't help overhearing your conversation. I wonder if I might offer a word of advice?'

Both Ruth and Angela stared at him.

'Remember they can't eat you,' he said.

Neither of them spoke, lips parted, eyes blank.

'I see so many girls. Unfortunately I can't tell them this, but if only they would think of me slipping on a banana skin, having my bath—well, it would make it easier for both of us. I hope you don't mind?'

'No,' Ruth said.

He leant back, pleased. The train snaked into the black station.

'Well,' he said, 'good luck. See you this evening, Reg.'

Both of them jumped from the moving train and disappeared.

'I suppose you know that man?' Angela asked bitterly. She was pressing herself back into the corner as though determined not to leave the train, as though she were going to be forced out of it.

'Of course not—'

'I suppose you've been gossiping about me with all your friends. I suppose everyone knows. I suppose everyone's dreadfully sorry for you—'

'Angela, don't be absurd. He thought you were—'

'I don't care what he thought! My God, I wish I'd done this by myself, I wish I'd gone to that woman, I wish I'd never even told you.' She jumped up, crying. '*You'd* never do it, you'd never go and see Fickstein or whatever his name is, you'd never go to some ghastly nursing home! It's all very well for you, you've never done anything like this in the whole of your life and you expect me to—' She stopped on a deep breath, wrenched open the carriage door and dropped clumsily on to the platform.

'Where are you going?' Ruth cried, scrambling after her. 'Where are you going?'

'To see the bloody doctor! That's what you want, isn't it?' She ran heavily away down the platform, pushing and struggling in her effort to escape from her mother.

'Harrods for lunch—' Ruth called, in a dying voice. It was like a bleat from another world, a bewildered cry of gentility and cosiness that carried no farther than the cloud of her breath in the cold air.

Chapter 32

'ABORTION,' Doctor Fickstein said, 'is illegal.'

'Yes,' Angela said. 'Yes, I know.'

He nodded, leaning far back in his chair, observing her over his steepled fingers. He had a sad, elongated face, smooth, colourless hair. She thought he was old, but in fact he was about fifty. Tinted photographs of a woman stood on the desk, which was otherwise empty except for a pink blotter and a green desk lamp.

'I do nothing illegal,' he said. 'I wish to make this perfectly clear.'

'All right,' Angela said. 'But whatever it is you do, let's get on with it. You've examined me, and you've got the letter. What happens next?'

'You're very impatient.'

'Of course I am. I want to get it over.'

'But we have not yet decided that we can, as you put it, get it over, have we?'

'Haven't we?'

'No.' He leant forward. If they were meek and grateful enough, he could trust them. This girl seemed to think she had a right to get rid of her child. She had yet to learn that you had no right to anything. She was, he thought wearily, a typical intellectual, under-developed and plain. She probably hadn't even enjoyed it.

A genuine pity for women had motivated his whole career, had filled his consulting-rooms in Vienna with some of the most exclusive pregnancies in Europe. Whether he delivered a living child or removed an embryo he always, afterwards, sent them flowers, bushes of thornless roses for the sad, soft, pretty creatures who had been disfigured by men. He persuaded them not to feed their babies, hating to see a breast misused; when he could, he tied their little Fallopian tubes into knots so that they need never suffer again. Persecution, danger, escape, internment had not changed this tender attitude. Women were his pets, to be protected against the ravages of childbirth and all ugliness. The sexual act itself was to him only tolerable when performed with so much technique, so much consideration and application to the right zones and climates and meridians that it resembled a safari rather than a necessary expression of love.

He had worked hard to establish himself in London after the war. Englishwoman were not always easy to love, English doctors were insensitive and vulgar and the English laws, which he must appear to observe, ridiculous. Every time he helped one of these unhappy girls he risked his entire career. In the private nursing homes he was treated with contempt, even with insolence. His patients were given the worst rooms, neglected by the nurses, despised by the matrons. And he, whose clinic in Vienna had been a model for the world, had to put up with it. For a pretty, tearful woman it was still worth it, but . . .

'You are not at all like your mother,' he said sadly.

Angela knew what he meant. She said nothing.

'I have yet to get the report of a psychologist, you understand.'

'I'd like to get it over before Christmas.'

'It will be necessary,' he said, with faint defiance, 'to get it over before Christmas. I am going away on December 26th. For a holiday.'

She looked at him with a flicker of interest. 'Oh, yes. I remember. When can I go and see this psychologist, then?'

'You seem very certain that his report will advise the termination of your pregnancy.'

'If you send me to him, of course it will.' She got up and pulled on her coat. 'I mean, it's all a lot of lies, isn't it? I'm perfectly healthy and I'm perfectly sane. There's no earthly reason why I shouldn't have this baby, except that I don't want to. Everyone knows that.'

'Everyone does not know that,' he said desperately. 'And if that is your attitude, I am afraid I shall be unable to undertake this case. My dear Miss Whiting, you must understand the *law.*'

'You mean you don't want to hear the truth? You don't even want to know it?'

'If you like to put it that way—yes.'

'But isn't that rather silly? After all,' she grinned at him quickly; he recognized a deep fear. 'After all, I'm putting my life in your hands.'

He smiled. 'In that case,' he said, 'I'm afraid I shall have you on my hands for a very long time.'

They both laughed quietly. She looked prettier, her hair less lank, her awkwardness rather touching.

'Now,' he said. 'I will send my report and Doctor Mac-Dermott's letter to the psychologist who usually deals with my patients. His name is Doctor Worbright, in Cornwall Place— Is anything the matter? You know him?'

'No. I just know someone who works in Cornwall Place. A dentist.'

'Well, that is hardly surprising. My secretary will let you know when Doctor Worbright can see you. And I think that is all.'

'Thank you.' She hesitated. She was aware for the first time that he was taking a risk. 'About the money—' she began clumsily.

'We will discuss that later.' He smiled directly into her eyes, which only a few moments ago had been hostile and honest. 'I think your mother said the young man would be responsible.'

'Yes.' She realised that she wanted to be attractive to him. His long face suddenly seemed beautiful and wise. His voice was romantic. She adorned him with all the qualities of sympathy and understanding with which, long ago, she had adorned the history mistress and the school chaplain. She wished she could talk to him about Tony. She had a momentary dream that Doctor Fickstein was in love with her.

'Well,' she said, plunging awkwardly away, 'thank you. Good-bye.'

When she had gone he sighed deeply and went back to his desk. He picked up MacDermott's letter, glanced at it, dropped it on the clean pink blotter. What foolishness. A girl of eighteen—she should have come to him years ago. Undoubtedly she had been inoculated against small pox. The chances of her becoming pregnant were a hundred times greater than the chances of her catching smallpox. The irresponsibility pained him. He really couldn't understand it. A curettage was not going to be so easy with this one: she was remarkably immature for her age. In any case it wasn't as easy as taking a simple and perfectly legal pre-caution—not to mention the expense, the risk, the emotional and psychological dangers involved where a girl had been brought up unprepared and unprotected. Yet the mother was so young. Nervous, certainly, but intelligent. Why had she allowed this to happen? Why?

He sat down, rubbing the back of his neck where the white collar cut into it, genuinely perplexed. He was, in an entirely unspiritual way, like a priest who cannot understand disbelief. It worried him that people could be so remarkably, so incomprehensibly, stupid. It made him sad.

The receptionist opened the door. 'Mrs. Bennett,' she said tersely. Even she despised him. He looked up and saw a heavy, middle-aged woman in a fur coat followed by a frightened girl. The girl was wearing a silly hat. Her mother's choice, no doubt. He smiled faintly. Abortion, Mrs. Bennett, is illegal. I wish to make this perfectly clear. I do nothing illegal.

'Good morning,' he sighed. 'Won't you please sit down—?'

Chapter 33

> '*God rest you merry, gentlemen,*
> *Let nothing you dismay*—'

THE CRIBS IN WOOLWORTH'S were hemmed in by unbreakable cows, unbreakable shepherds. A reckless obsession with cleanliness crammed the shops with loads of soap, quarries of bath-salts, oceans of essence and perfume, novelty face cloths and novelty sponges and enterprising, effervescent, energising chemicals and soap, more and more, to wash away the sins of the world. Betty Johnson went to stay with her mother in Deal and the British Railways van drove frequently across the Common with trunks sent Luggage in Advance, locked, ominous, containing useful blotters and painfully embroidered tray-cloths.

Miss de Beer cut her finger with the bread knife. If she died, she said, there would be no one to go to the funeral.

'I got you a small present, Maxine. It's for Christmas, really.'

'For Christmas? But Christmas is weeks away, Rex! . . . Oh, Rex, you shouldn't have—'

'Well—I thought you might like them.'

'But you shouldn't spend your money on me, really you shouldn't, it makes me feel *awful.*'

'Aren't you going to put them on?'

'Later. I'll put them on in a little while.'

'I got them at Aspreys.'

'Oh, Rex, you shouldn't have. I'd like to give you a great big kiss— No, dear, not *here*. Please.'

'I thought we might go back and have dinner at the flat, make ourselves comfortable—'

'Let's see how we feel, shall we? Cheers. Merry Christmas.'

'God, I'm dreading it.'

'Now you're not to talk like that. You'll have all the children.'

'Only two.'

'Well, and Angela. She's only a child really. Just think, you'll be able to give them a tree and all those pretty things on it and presents. And stockings. Do they have stockings?'

'I don't know.'

'Well, you should know! You should dress up as Santa Claus. Daddy always did. You'd make a lovely Santa Claus.'

'There's no need to be bitchy.'

'I'm not. I'm just thinking what a lovely time you'll have while I'm all alone in London. It's not much fun for me, all alone.'

'You won't be.'

'Well, of course I shall. What do you mean, I won't be?'

'You'll find someone. That ghastly Herb. Someone.'

'Oh, Rex, don't be so *silly*. Let's have another drink. I wish they had some music in this place. It's the dullest bar in London, I'm quite sure of that.'

'I'm sorry. We'll go somewhere else.'

'Where?'

'Well, there are plenty of bars.'

'I know there are plenty of bars.'

'What's to stop you going to them, then? I haven't seen you for three days. What have you been doing? Sitting at home knitting?'

'No, I haven't.'

'What have you been doing, then? What?'

'Oh, Rex, don't shout at me. You're being perfectly silly.'

'I'm sorry.'

'Cheers.'

'Cheers.'

'As it happened, I met Herb this morning.'

'Oh.'

'He knows someone who's casting a telly play. It's all about juvenile delinquents and there's this girl. He thinks I'd do for the part. He says I don't look a day over eighteen and she's meant to be eighteen. You know—I'd wear my hair back in a pony tail and I've got good bones, thank goodness. Anyway, I'm seeing the producer tomorrow.'

'Oh. Good.'

'It's not much money, of course, but it's a lovely part. You can put feeling in it. You know, really live it. This girl's mother tries to put her on the streets, but of course she won't. So it turns out that teen-agers are really much better than their parents even if they do rock and roll and everything. Herb says it's a very specific play written in the manner of Paddy Chayefsky.'

'Oh.'

'You don't know who Paddy Chayefsky is, do you?'

'No. And I can't say I care, much.'

'Obviously you don't. You don't care about anything much, do you?'

'No, except taking you back to the flat for a good—'

'Oh, Rex! I can't ever talk to you. I can't ever say anything to you. You just treat me as though I was a—child, or something.'

'Well, what do you want to talk about?'

'Oh, I don't *know* what I want to talk about.'

'Talk away if you want to. I'm listening.'

'You're not listening! You don't understand a word I say. I'm very sensitive, and—'

'You mean that Herb says you're very sensitive.'

'Well, he does. I was sensitive with you, wasn't I? You said I understood you. Well, I was sorry for you.'

'Sorry for me? Good God. What for?'

'You know perfectly well what for. Because you have a crazy wife and no home to go to—'

'You don't know what you're talking about. You'd better finish that drink and we'll go back to the flat.'

'Listen to you!'

'Why, what's wrong?'

'Honestly, Rex . . . Oh, do stop pawing me all the time.'

'Just tell me you like me. Go on. Tell me something nice.'

'Oh, stop it. For Pete's sake, stop it. Just buy me another drink.'

'You can have one if you tell me— Maxine! Maxine! Wait. I didn't mean it.'

'Buy me a drink, then.'

'All right. I'm sorry. I'll buy you a drink.'

> *'O come, all ye faithful,*
> *Joyful and triumphant,*
> *O come ye, O come ye*
> *To Bethlehem—'*

The veterans trumpeted up and down Ramsbridge High Street, the onslaught became louder, angrier, only ten more shopping days, eighty shopping hours. The wreath was delivered for the Tanners' front door and Baby expressed a number of sweet notions about Jesus which she had learnt from the German help, who burnt a new candle for each day of Advent and littered her room with wilting branches of Tannenbaum.

'Oh, God, he's at his worst. I can't stand it. I promise you I can't. Why does he have to shout all the time?'

'Hush—'

'Why should I hush? Just because he's my father it doesn't give him the right to—'

'You don't want him to think there's anything wrong, do you?'

'What are you both mumbling about now? What's wrong with you? What's happened? What?'

'Nothing's happened.'

'What have you done to your hair? Makes you look like a sick schoolmistress. Why don't you wash it or something?'

'Shut up! Shut up! Shut up!'

'Now what have I said? What have I said wrong now?'

'Nothing, Rex. Nothing.'

' "Nothing, nothing, nothing!" Maybe you don't exist? Maybe this whole house is just a figment of my imagination? I come home tired after a week's work, I come home—'

'I'm sorry.'

'Well, I don't mean to be bad-tempered. It's just that I can't stand her hanging about. Always hanging about. Never doing anything.'

'I think—I think she may be going away for Christmas.'

198

'What? Angela?'

'Yes, she—'

'Where? Who with? She's not starting up any nonsense with that boy, is she?'

'What do you mean?'

'I suppose that hasn't occurred to you? You'd be perfectly happy to let her go off with some boy. You wouldn't even ask. Just let her go and be vaguely surprised when she came back pregnant. Where's she going? Who's she going with?'

'I—I don't know, it isn't fixed, it's—'

'Well, she can't go. What about the boys? It's Christmas. Can't she stay with her own family at Christmas? Tell her she can't go.'

'Why don't you tell her?'

'Yes. Well. Well, we'll wait and see. For heaven's sake, why do you keep nagging me all the time? What's happened?'

'Nothing's happened, Rex. I keep telling you. Nothing.'

> *'Once in Royal David's City,*
> *Stood a lowly cattle shed—'*

'Why must they play the same things, the same things all the time?'

'You don't have to have the wireless on all day.' But if it wasn't the wireless it was the veterans or the carol singers or Miss de Beer fluting a sad contralto from the kitchen.

'What else is there to listen to? Beer talking about her relatives? You ticking off lists all the time? God, one's got to have *something*—'

But there is something, Ruth wanted to shout, knowing it would be a lie. Angela carried the child in her body; Ruth carried it in her imagination. To Angela it was a use-

199

less growth, already dead. To Ruth it was an image, unformed, folded and wrapped in itself, concerned only with
survival. Her imagination built protective walls round her
idea of the child. She dreamed about it at night, an un-
troublesome, unapprehensive midget, fully dressed and
adult, smiling at her over the rim of a gigantic table. 'She
won't be any trouble,' she told Rex. 'She's already grown-
up.' These dreams disgusted her, because in them the child
was her's and Angela did not exist.

'It's ten days since you saw Fickstein.'

'I know.'

'Hadn't I better ring him up?'

'Why should *you* ring him up? Anyway, he rang me
yesterday.'

'Oh. You didn't tell me.'

'I know.'

'Well . . . what did he say?'

Angela fiddled with the radio. Between Jingle Bells and
Religion for Schools the air was filled with frenetic screams,
the apparent destruction of space.

'He said I'm to go and see Worbright on Wednesday.'

'Worbright?'

'Oh, he's the psychologist. I *told* you. Really, you don't
remember a thing.'

'Well . . . what time on Wednesday?'

'Eleven. But I can go by myself.'

'The boys arrive on Wednesday. Their train gets in at
half-past twelve.'

'I don't see what difference that makes. I've told you. I
can go by myself.'

'I meant—that I shall be going up to London, anyway.'

She looked round Angela's room. The bed was unmade,

the table littered with books and papers and dirty cups, the dressing-table bare, the waste-paper basket overflowing. It was a cold, hated room in which nothing was worth bothering about, nothing was ever finished. Ruth felt her arms move, open in a hopeless gesture of pity.

'So if you like, I could come—'

'It doesn't make any difference. Come if you like. I don't care.'

'I'm sorry. I'm sorry. I wish I could—'

'You're being wonderful. Why don't you leave me alone?'

She snapped on the radio again, turning it full volume.

> 'God rest you merry, gentlemen,
> Let nothing you dismay—'

Ruth turned it off. In the silence there seemed nothing to say. There was, after all, no comfort for either of them. They looked at each other, startled and uneasy.

'I'll help you make your bed,' Ruth said, turning away. But she did it alone, as though it were a punishment.

Chapter 34

T HERE'S ANOTHER THING I didn't tell you,' Angela said.

Ruth looked enquiring. It was all she could manage. She brightened her eyes, lifted her mouth a little, inclined her head to one side. Rebellion against these tricks of tact and sensitivity burned inside her. She did not ask what it was.

'He hangs out in Cornwall Place. This Doctor Worbright.'

'Oh.' Rex carried on his practice in Cornwall Place. It was a short, wide street so overpopulated with doctors, dentists, psychiatrists and occulists that many of them saw their clients in partitioned cubicles or holes under the stairs; the waiting-rooms were a confusion of psychosomatic illnesses which anyone picked at random from the brass plates outside could probably have cured. It was not, therefore, remarkable that Doctor Worbright practised in Cornwall Place. 'Which number?' she asked, pretending not to see the point.

'Thirty-seven.'

'Then at least,' Ruth said cheerfully, 'it's on the other side of the street.'

'I thought you wouldn't come if you knew.'

'Is that why you didn't tell me? Or why you did?'

Angela looked away. At last she mumbled, 'You had a letter from Tony this morning, didn't you?'

'Yes.' She had it in her handbag now, as they sat opposite each other in the familiar train. She should have destroyed it, but in some obscure way this seemed too merciful. They were alone in the carriage and she was afraid that her anger would become uncontrollable, if she once allowed herself to speak. She tightened her fingers over the clasp of her handbag and looked out of the window.

'What—what did he say?'

'Nothing. Nothing, really.'

'Was it about the money?'

'Partly.' Then she added quickly, imploring, 'Hasn't he written to you?'

'Oh, yes. He writes. I just thought—'

'And what does he say to you?'

'Oh . . . that he's sorry. You know.'

'And what do you think about that?'

'Why do you want to know what I think all the time? You didn't used to. Why are you always getting at me?'

Ruth levelled her voice. 'I want to know what you think. That's all. It would be easier.'

'Well, if you want to know, I don't think anything! I just don't think anything! I don't have any point of view, you see? It's no good wanting me to have. I just don't!' She had begun to shout, twisting her cold, ungloved hands together.

'Is that what you're going to tell Doctor Worbright?'

'Oh, I don't know what I'm going to tell Doctor Worbright!'

As usual they came to an abrupt halt in front of a wall of silence. Ruth undid her handbag and took out the letter.

'Do you want to see it?' she asked gently.

'I don't care.'

'Please read it if you want to.'

Angela snatched the letter, pulled it out of the envelope and began to read. Ruth watched her, but her face did not change, showed no disgust. She read slowly, with her mouth slightly open, like a child.

Dear Mrs. Whiting,

I must sincerely apologise for not having written to you before this, but I have been extremely busy and, as you can well imagine, burdened with the worry of this most unfortunate situation. I must say at once that I am only too well aware of my responsibility in this matter, and I am also painfully conscious of the worry I have brought on you and your family. However, I am sure you will appreciate my meaning when I say that I cannot be altogether sorry, since it is a wonderful thing to think of a new life coming into being, even if the circumstances are such that it must unhappily be terminated, and this has been a considerable comfort to me in the past weeks and I hope that you may feel the same.

I am afraid that as things stand I must most regretfully ask you to meet the cost of the operation initially, and I will of course repay you as soon as I possibly can. The reason for this is that my friend, from whom I hoped to obtain the money, is at the moment unable to lend it to me as he has decided to leave Oxford and take up writing as a career, which will not of course be immediately profitable. If my father knew about this situation I should have to leave home and get a job, as he is in many ways a bigoted and narrow-minded man and although he would probably give me the money if I told him the position I would feel it impossible to go on depending on him any longer. I will do this and give up the University if it is necessary to avoid giving Angela an unwanted child and getting you into financial difficulties, but I hope it is understandable that my career at Oxford is of great importance to me and that I want to try out all other possibilities before going to such an extreme length.

I must say that I feel that if Angela would tell Mr. Whiting about the position, it would make everything much easier for all of us, as he is clearly the most reasonable and sympathetic father, quite unlike my own. I have suggested this to her a number of times, but perhaps under the circumstances it would be a help if you could use your influence in the matter. I do most earnestly ask you not to think that I am trying to avoid my responsibility, but I am sure you will see that as matters stand it is practically impossible for me to obtain the money immediately without risking my entire career, and I am sure Mr. Whiting would appreciate this.

Finally, I would again like to say how extremely sorry I am for putting you to all this trouble. I feel in a way that justice has been done, for while it is undoubtedly most painful and worrying for Angela she can at least deal with the situation in a practical way, whereas I must bear it alone and also bear my feeling of helplessness, which is quite overwhelming.

Yours very sincerely,

Anthony Bateman.

Angela folded the letter slowly, fitted it back in the envelope and handed it to Ruth. 'Well?' she asked. 'Have you got the money?' She was serious, but not distressed.

'No,' Ruth said. She held the letter, uncertain what to do with it. 'Do you want to tell him?'

'Daddy? Good heavens, no. That would be the end.'

Ruth dropped the letter into her handbag. 'Then what,' she asked, 'do you think we're going to do?'

'I don't know.' She lit up with eagerness. 'Can't you borrow it from someone?'

'Who?'

'Oh, I don't know. The Tanners. Jane Tanner. They've got pots of money, haven't they? Or what about the Rackworth man, he's absolutely rolling and after all, he must *know*—'

'No,' Ruth said.

'What?'

'I mean I can't.'

'Why not?'

'Because—' She had taken a deep breath, certain that the reason would be clear and unanswerable. It wasn't. The breath hovered and came out in a short, exasperated sigh. 'Because I won't,' she said.

'You won't?' Angela stared, her eyes filling with tears. 'You mean you really wouldn't, even if there was no other way?'

Ruth shook her head. She was stubborn; even, for a moment, cruel. In fact she still had the money that Rex had given her for Antibes. He would remember this soon, but in the meanwhile she could spend it, it was hers. Why not, since she was so unreliable? Don't worry, darling. I can condone your abortion, arrange it, even pay for it.

But she was struggling under the weight, permitting herself one ineffectual gesture. 'Why won't you tell Rex?' she asked angrily. 'Why?'

'But you know why!' The girl was bewildered. Nothing, no one was dependable. Her mother was a complete stranger. 'Because you just couldn't, I mean you know you couldn't, you can't tell him anything—'

'Have you ever tried?'

'Have you?'

It was the vicious, accurate retort of an adult woman. For the first time Ruth could have said, 'Yes, when I told him about you.' Her hands, rigidly pressed together, loosened, wandered vaguely across her lap, smoothing it. She felt dizzy, as though she had just stepped back from a cliff edge, the end of the world. After a few minutes she said hesitantly, 'Don't worry about the money. I'm sure we can arrange it.'

'Good.'

They didn't speak again until the train pulled into Paddington, but the tension between them was, in some curious way, relaxed. In the taxi going to Cornwall Place they chattered, furtive, as though they were a little drunk.

'Well, if we do see him we'll have to think of something—'

'Well, we'll have to say we were going to see him, that's all.'

'Anyway, he'll be busy drilling away at some duchess. Probably we'll bump into that awful Craxton. That would be worse.'

'I don't see how we could explain it, I mean being in Cornwall Place.'

'We could make up something. We could tell him it's you.'

'What do you mean?'

'Tell him *you're* pregnant. Why not? That would solve the whole thing, money and all. I mean, he wouldn't want you to have a baby *now*, would he?'

For a moment the balance, toppling high above reality, was lost. There was nothing but horror. Ruth twitched her mouth wider; smiled. 'What a brilliant idea.'

'Isn't it?' Having triumphed, although she did not quite know why or over what, Angela felt generous. 'And, after all,' she said, 'it's not impossible. I mean, it could quite easily be true, couldn't it?'

The taxi stopped. Ruth saw Craxton's car parked by the curb. She looked up at the long, first-floor window.

'Come on,' Angela said. 'Do come on.'

But Ruth was deliberately slow about paying the driver. Even when he had driven away she stood on the pavement putting away her change, silver in one compartment of her purse, coppers in another, tucking the purse down into her handbag, shutting it, hanging it over her wrist before she turned and walked up the steps. The door was already open, Angela waiting impatiently inside. Ruth looked back again from the doorway as though inviting Rex, almost willing him to come to the window. Someone was unconscious in there, Craxton had dabbed the arm, plunged in the needle, waited while his confident smile grew remote, became confused with eternity. Rex was working, extracting some small, decayed bone. Eternity would dwindle to him; he would be waiting, patient and reassuring, for the confusion to pass; he would be at the end of it. For a moment, as the window remained empty, she felt like running across the street, breaking in on this monstrous intimacy. Craxton came out of the house and ran down the steps, stooped to unlock the door of his car. She hurried after Angela, down the dark hall.

Chapter 35

HAD MY GREEN COAT,' the woman said plaintively. She was wearing Persian lamb and' four rows of pearls tight round her thin neck. 'I had my green coat on when I left this morning, I know I did. Do you think I left it at the hairdresser's?'

'I don't know,' her friend said. She looked tired and wore a maroon felt hat and tweed suit, the uniform of a good, kind woman. 'We could always telephone.'

'But I couldn't have left it at the hairdresser's, could I? I mean, what would I have been wearing when I came out?'

'Let's look at *The Tatler*,' the friend said. The woman pulled disconsolately at her pearls and looked at Ruth, who was waiting.

'I suppose I might have put it down somewhere,' she said.

'Look,' the friend said eagerly, 'here's a picture of Bunty.'

'Not a very good one.'

'No—' the friend said judicially. 'No, not good at all. Her nose isn't like that.'

'Oh, her nose is all right. It's the eyes.'

'Yes, there's something wrong with the eyes.'

'I didn't leave it in the hall, did I?'

'We already asked, dear. They say they haven't seen it.'

The woman sat back, nibbling the knuckle of her thumb. Her glance, dark, bright, wary, shot from side to side of the gloomy room as though to catch something.

'Did I leave it in here,' she asked, 'when we came in?'

'No, dear. You weren't wearing your green coat when we came here.'

'What was I wearing then?'

For the first time, the friend glanced at Ruth. 'You were wearing what you've got on,' she said brightly. 'Such a pretty coat.'

'This?' The woman held a piece of her coat between her finger and thumb, unbelieving.

'Yes, dear. Oh, look, here's the Bridgely point-to-point. Do look, there's Alison.'

'Alison who?'

'Alison Blount-Montagu. Her sister married that Greek, don't you remember?'

'I'm so tired.'

'Yes, dear, well in a minute or two we'll get a taxi. When you're feeling quite steady.'

'I'm so tired,' the woman repeated heavily. She was about Ruth's age, perhaps younger. She wore a wedding ring and her nails were very long, smoothly painted. Hungry, suspicious, tired out, she scoured the room with her brilliant eyes. 'Fortnums,' she said. 'Perhaps I left it there. We were there for coffee, weren't we?'

'No, dear. That was last week.'

'Where did we have coffee today, then?'

'We didn't have any, because your appointment was at half-past ten today. Now let's just see if we can find Annabel's wedding, shall we?' She leafed the magazine as though Annabel were gaily hiding from her, like a woman keeping a difficult child up to the mark, a woman passionately believing in good behaviour. The anxious one lost faith and interest when Annabel couldn't be found. Her eyes returned to Ruth, a hard, brilliant stare.

'It is perfectly maddening,' she said, 'when you lose anything of value. It was my favourite coat. Now,' she twitched her shoulders restlessly, 'it's gone.'

Ruth smiled, but only slightly, because she was not sure whether she was being spoken to.

'I think we could go now,' the friend said. 'Do you feel up to it now?'

'I feel all right.'

'Then I'll just see about the taxi.' She went out, leaving the door ajar. The woman leant forward, speaking rapidly.

'Would you ask them? I know it must be here. I was wearing it when I came. A green coat. They've hung it up somewhere and forgotten, you know there are so many people here. It's not that I mind, but I won't be lied to. You understand?'

'Yes,' Ruth said.

'I hate dishonesty.'

'Yes.'

'You see. You're telling me the truth. It's not difficult. I was wearing that green coat when I left the house this morning.'

'Then you left it,' Ruth said, 'in the place where you changed into that one.'

'Did I?' Again she plucked at the Persian lamb. 'Do you think I did?'

'Yes,' Ruth said.

'You seem very certain.'

'It's only that if you were wearing the green one, and

now you're wearing that one, you must have changed them somewhere.'

'Changed them over, you mean?'

'Yes.'

'Yes. I see.'

The friend came back, ready to grapple with her. The woman got up. She sniggered softly, gathering her gloves and handbag.

'You know what a fool I am,' she said. 'It was last week I wore the green coat. That was why I thought I'd left it in Fortnums. Why didn't you tell me?'

The friend blushed; the blush poured down her neck, inside the collar of her crêpe blouse. 'The taxi's here, dear. I shouldn't worry about the coat any more, if I were you.'

'I only want to know why you didn't tell me?'

The friend looked as though she were going to cry. She was caught in a clinging, invisible web. She seemed to be stifling. What good was kindness? She moved her thick arms, stamped her feet twice as though she were cold, or testing the solidity of the floor. 'The taxi,' she said, 'is waiting, Bridget.'

The woman smiled quickly at Ruth. 'You see?' she asked. She went out quickly. Ruth was left with her own smile fixed and meaningless, a signal made too late.

I was like that. I could be like that again. Oh, no, I'll never be like that again.

Why not? All this hasn't made any real difference. The baby will be thrown away. Angela will go back. The children will go back. One evening, in a few weeks' time, you will drive home. The house will be empty. It will be winter. You will be older.

But it will be different.

Why?

Because I'm nearer to Angela. I've almost caught her up.

But Angela won't be there. It's too late. She's gone. You're alone.

But Julian and Mike—I love them.

It's too late for that too. Everyone's gone away. This child isn't yours, you know.

I know that. I know that.

You don't. You're making yourself believe the child is yours. That it's going to be born. That it's going to grow. That you're going to walk with it across the Common. You're pretending it will be there for the rest of your life. Not Angela, not Julian or Mike, but this child.

I'm not. I'm not.

It could be yours. It's not impossible. It could quite easily be true.

It couldn't. I don't want it. It's going to be dead.

Yes, it's going to be dead. And then what will you do? What will you do then? The house will be empty. It will be winter. You will be older.

But it will be different.

Why?

Because . . . Oh, why doesn't she come? What on earth is she telling him?

She got up and walked across the room to the window. She pulled back the net curtain and looked across the street. Nothing. She looked at her watch, thought of calling a taxi, felt agitated about getting to Waterloo in time. She went back to the window again. The long white curtains on the first-floor window moved, were held by Rex looking down into the street, stroking his chin, feeling up the side of his cheek. He was talking to someone, but looking along the street, expecting someone else. He turned his head slightly and seemed to look directly at her. She raised her hand with the hesitant, almost coy gesture of someone surprised in a hiding place. He glanced at his watch, let the curtain drop.

'What on earth are you doing?' Angela asked.

'What a long time you've been. Hours.'

'Twenty-five minutes, actually. I think I convinced him I'm balmy enough. Anyway, he says he'll get in touch with Fickstein.' She looked fat and contented, as though Worbright had given her a good meal.

'What was he like?'

'Oh, a scruffy little man, but bliss to talk to. Imagine being paid for that. By the way, I told him to send you the bill, I hope that's all right.'

'All right,' Ruth said.

'I'll ask them to get a taxi, shall I?'

'Yes, all right.'

Angela put her arm round Ruth's shoulders. 'Sorry you were bored,' she said and hugged her, urgently needing to express delight and to make up for thinking, as she came back into the room and saw Ruth standing by the window like a child on a rainy day—how insignificant she looks, how stupid.

Chapter 36

SPLENDID, THE BOYS SAID, look at that super Jag, I say, have our trunks come, I say, how perfectly splendid. Like eager stockbrokers, Ruth thought, looking amazed at their haircuts, their enormous hands. 'Like a couple of ghastly queers,' Angela said with disgust. She had always preferred Mike to Julian because he was smaller and used to seem fond of her. Now they were indistinguishable, a dreadful noise.

'Do you have to shout *all* the time?' she asked, despairing.

'They aren't shouting,' Ruth said, deafened.

'We built a splendid glider—'

'Oh, a shocking business. It didn't glide an inch.'

'Can we go to the Boat Show?'

'Have our reports come?'

'I say, old Angela's getting shockingly fat, isn't she?'

'I'm in the choir,' Mike said modestly. 'I sang a solo.'

'Yes,' Angela said. 'I can believe that.'

Unexpectedly, Miss de Beer was a success. It was difficult to understand her appeal, except that she reassured them with a certain manliness, a lack of subtlety. She welcomed them with tea, weighty rock cakes and apple pie, two loaves of bread and butter and suspicious potted meat she had made herself. Angela went to her bedroom, saying she couldn't bear it. For the first time, Ruth felt fond of Miss de Beer, sat at the table like a visitor while the black tea was poured out, smiled nervously, watched the bread disappear.

'It's nice to have children about,' Miss de Beer said, energetically washing up. 'It's not Christmas without children, is it? I thought I'd make a cake tomorrow, that'll leave me time for mince pies on Monday. They like cocoa for supper, I'm sure.'

'Oh, yes,' Ruth said. 'They love cocoa.'

They were out in the dark with their bicycles. They had dragged out the bagatelle, looted the tidy cupboard, begun to play ping-pong, pinned up a picture of some girl in a bikini—why?—left all the lights on. The radio blared and the house, with all its doors except Angela's open, had a startled look, gaping with shock. The telephone rang and Julian dashed through the kitchen into the hall, shouting, 'I'll answer it.' Ruth waited on the stairs. 'It's some man,' he said. 'For you.'

She went down and smiled at him cheerfully as she took the receiver. He waited, hanging about, his hair damp.

'Yes?'

'Mrs. Whiting?'

She immediately recognised the quiet murmur. She glanced at Julian and put her hand over the mouthpiece. 'Where's Mike?'

He shrugged, leaning against the wall, looking vaguely towards the kitchen. She couldn't tell him to go away. She turned her back on him, as though this would conceal something.

'Yes,' she said. 'Speaking.'

'Doctor Fickstein here. I have heard from Doctor Worbright this afternoon and now I hope I shall be able to make the necessary arrangements.'

'Yes,' she said. 'When?'

'It is not always easy to find a bed.'

'No, but you're going away—'

'On Thursday.'

'So,' she glanced hopelessly at Julian, 'it must be before then?'

'Of course. It will be Tuesday at the latest. You would be able to bring her up to London on Tuesday?'

But that's Christmas Eve, she thought stupidly, how can I? 'Yes, of course. But you see, it's a little difficult—'

'Naturally.' He cut her short, not wanting to know. 'It has taken longer than I thought, owing to the delay at the start.'

'The delay?'

'You had difficulty, you remember, in contacting your doctor.'

'Yes.' She took the responsibility. 'I know. It can't be helped, I know that.'

'I expected to see you again, to discuss the question of the fee. I believe you said this was arranged?'

'Yes, I—'

'It will be a hundred and fifty guineas, or in that region. I do not like to spring surprises.'

'And the—the place?'

'I have not yet found the place,' he said stiffly.

'No, I mean how much will it be?'

'From fifteen to thirty guineas, it is hard to say.'

'Would you hold on a minute?' She covered the mouthpiece again and turned to Julian. 'Would you find Mike,' she said, 'and go up to your bath now?'

He scuffed off down the corridor, dragging his feet. She watched him swing round on the bottom of the banisters and start, incredibly slowly, up the stairs.

'I'm sorry,' she said. 'How long—how long will she be there?'

'If everything is straightforward,' he said, 'not more than a couple of days.'

'And if it isn't?'

'We do not count our chickens before they are hatched,' he said, with what might have been vile humour. 'I think it will be quite straightforward. Please do not worry the girl at all.'

'No. Of course not. You'll let me know, then?'

'I will let you know.'

She looked frantically at the telephone, frantically towards the stairs. She could see one black shoe and a relaxed leg swinging over the banisters.

'Darling, what *are* you doing?' It was a particular note of exasperation, guilty and soft, without courage.

'Waiting.' Julian was lying stomach down on the banisters, as though in bed.

'But what for?'

'Mike.'

'But why—?'

The telephone rang again. She hurried back, as though to muffle it.

'That was a hell of a long conversation,' Rex said.

'What was?'

'You've been engaged for the past quarter of an hour.'

'Oh. I'm sorry. Do you want to—?'

'Who was it, anyway?'

Julian let go, arrived elegantly on the hall floor. He looked suddenly dejected, as though missing something.

'Julian's here,' she said. 'Do you want to talk to him?' Without waiting for an answer she held out the receiver and said, 'It's Daddy. He wants to talk to you.' Julian came eagerly. He's glad, Ruth thought. He wants to talk to Rex. Mike came out of the kitchen with his mouth full.

'She makes splendid tarts,' he said, and leaned up against Ruth as though she were a gate, feet crossed, cheek bulging, hands in pockets. She held his shoulders to steady herself.

'I don't know,' Julian was saying, in his polite, shrill voice. 'Some man.' He turned towards Ruth. 'Who was it on the 'phone, Mum?'

She blinked. 'No one,' she said. She pushed Mike forward a little. 'We'll go upstairs.'

'I want to talk to him too,' Mike said, relaxing against her. She put her hand on his bristly hair, like touching a hedgehog.

'Oh, perfectly splendid,' Julian was saying, 'thanks awfully . . . Are you coming down tomorrow? . . . Yes, jolly good. Here, Mike wants to talk to you—' He gave the receiver to Mike, who took it gingerly. 'Hullo. Daddy? This is Mike. Oh yes, super, thanks awfully . . .'

Abruptly, without warning, Ruth's eyes filled with tears. Her eyes burned, as though the tears were acid. She turned her head away and stumbled into the sitting-room. In the firelight every metallic object wavered and glistened. She stood rigid, head bent, injuring her hands in the effort to subdue any sound. She heard Mike ring off, but they didn't come in. They were whispering, uncertain what to do, where to go. She had no handkerchief and scrubbed her face on her sleeve. When she stepped out into the passage they were waiting for her, but did not look at her. They did not look at Angela either, advancing lugubriously along the hall. They appeared very awkward, interrupted in their muttering by the two women, cut off from their own world.

'He's got me an air gun,' Julian mumbled, hunching his shoulders.

'How perfectly splendid,' Ruth said. She held them lightly, guiding them past Angela as though, in passing, there might be some slight danger.

Chapter 37

Tuesday?' Angela asked. 'But that's Christmas Eve.'

'I know. It might be before. It might be Monday.'

There was a long silence. 'Well,' Angela said. She looked at Ruth's dressing-table with the vacant interest of someone in a museum. Then she moved slowly on to the open wardrobe, the chest of drawers, scanning them. 'What are we going to say?'

'I'll think of something. Haven't you got a friend, I mean a girl?'

'Not really.' Her back turned, she investigated the musical box with the tip of one finger.

'Well, we'll think of something.'

'And the money? Don't they want it before—?'

'I shouldn't think so. Anyway, don't worry.'

There was another silence, then she said abruptly, 'Well, good night, then.' Her school bedroom slippers slapped quickly down the corridor and her door closed.

The next morning the Common looked as though it had been opened to the public. Bicycles wavered across it at an early hour, the blue winter day tinkled with bells and thin cries; trees shook and the gardeners took refuge in their huts while branches of holly and fir were slashed and dragged indoors. The dead bracken was trampled again and a red kite danced in the sky like a storm signal. The clean black cars, instead of backing swiftly out of their garages and hurrying away, backed, stopped, turned, stopped again, waiting for some child to find what it had lost, remember what it had forgotten. The women wore shining and distracted smiles. Such fun, they called, as they passed each other without pausing for enquiry or coffee or news of the foreign helps. Such fun to have them home again, isn't it? The helps were rushed off their feet, had no time to talk to each other on the telephone, grew mutinous and longed for home. Jane Tanner kept Baby indoors. They sat together by the fire in a state of siege and every time the door opened jumped with alarm. Rackworth's Jaguar was seen speeding across the Common with a great Christmas tree lashed to the boot. The pale, set faces of the passengers, their dark clothes, made it look like a getaway.

By teatime only a slight lassitude had descended. Most of the men returning home that evening would stay for ten days. The women ran about in a fluster, like nuns forced on a secular outing. Between their husbands and their children they didn't know where they were. The quantities of food made them, used to cream cheese and water biscuits, ill. They were agitated at the prospect of having to explain themselves, of having to live in public for so long. As the time of arrival came nearer they telephoned each other, breathlessly, as though for the last time.

'We must meet . . . keep in touch . . . Come for drinks . . . Yes, do keep in touch . . . Yes, do—'

The men arrived rowdy with the spirit of Christmas.

All of them had assumed a dazzling Pickwickian appearance, rubbed their hands and hit their sons on the back, roared 'Merry Christmas' and kicked the fires and opened the port and left parcels about for their wives to hide away. They were going to enjoy themselves, by God, they were going to relax. The moment of disillusion gaped in front of them. Unseeing, they kept their balance like clowns on the edge of a crevasse.

'We'll follow the hunt on Boxing Day,' Rex said. He had already promised the boys the pantomime, a shooting party, driving lessons and a good ten-mile tramp. They were bright with pleasure.

'Gosh,' they said, 'splendid.' They hung round him, followed him about the room, treated him as though he were a hero.

'We'll take your mother and sister too. Do them good. We'll make up a party. What?'

The boys glanced at each other, nodded obediently.

Ruth said quickly, 'Oh, we'd spoil it, I'm sure.'

The boys looked happier.

'Of course you wouldn't.' He expanded in front of the fire, smiled encouragingly at Angela. 'Angela would like you to come. We'll make up a party.'

'I'm afraid,' Angela said, without raising her eyes from her book, 'that I shan't be here, anyway.'

The silence was too short, it hardly gave Ruth time to take a breath. Rex had become rigid, petrified in his generous gesture. 'You mean,' he asked ponderously, 'that you intend to spend your Christmas elsewhere?'

'That's right.' She turned a page. Only Ruth noticed that her hand was shaking.

'And might I ask where?'

'Certainly. With a friend. Her name is Phyllis Brigson and she lives with her grandmother in Lichfield.' She glanced up, as though to assure herself that this was sufficient. 'Lichfield,' she added unnecessarily, 'is in Staffordshire, I think.'

He turned uncertainly to Ruth.

'Do you know anything about this?'

'Oh, yes,' Ruth said, too eagerly. 'I told you before—'

'Then since it's all been settled without my knowledge,' he smiled bleakly, putting his hand on Mike's shoulder, 'there's nothing more to say, is there? Who's going to win at ping-pong?'

He had survived it. The boys towed him upstairs like a trophy. Angela put down her book. 'Well,' she said, 'that went off all right.'

'Yes. Who is Phyllis Brigson?'

'She doesn't exist. I mean, I made her up. She obviously fixed him, though.' A child's grin briefly sharpened her face.

There was no longer anything wrong with lying. It had become, like killing in wartime, not only necessary but honourable. It was absurd to feel any distaste for it.

'You don't disapprove, do you?' Angela asked slyly. 'What else could I have said?'

'Nothing.'

'It was a brilliant success, anyway. Why do you think he took it so calmly?'

'Oh, I don't know.' She felt suffocated in the over-heated room. She opened a window, leaving it gaping, the curtain clumsily drawn aside. 'Because of the boys, I expect.'

'He's very fond of them, isn't he?'

'Of course. Of course he is.'

'But he's never been fond of me.'

'Oh, Angela—'

'No. I don't mind. I only wonder why.'

'Of course he's fond of you!' Ruth said vehemently. It occurred to her that dishonesty had never been unconscious, accidental; it had always, as now, been deliberate, the only way of survival. The opportunity to speak the truth, to use the language taught you in childhood, never arose.

'Oh, well,' Angela said, shrugging, returning to her book, 'you know it's not true. Never mind.'

That night, when the light was switched out, Ruth felt the whole of his heavy body restless, moving uneasily in the bed beside her. She lay still, but curiously feeble, unwilling to sleep.

'Tired?' he asked.

She moved her head slightly. Years ago, this question had meant should they make love. Only two answers were possible, yes or no. For Rex, uncertainty had been the same as refusal. 'Tired?' he would demand, before touching her. Now, uncertain what he meant, she said nothing.

'It's a pity about Angela. Can't see why she wants to go away for Christmas.'

'Oh, well—' Her hand, falling open, touched his. He did not move.

'I've been looking forward to this Christmas, having the boys back. What?'

'I didn't say anything. I'm glad.'

They were silent again. She didn't move, and yet she had the feeling that her body had moved towards him. Her hand lay open, her lips parted. In this weakness and peace there could be, if not an act of love, then a gesture of forgiveness. If she moved or spoke, the spell—for it was like a transla-

226

tion into water, into weed, into something drifting without substance—would be broken, there would be nothing. The feeling, a longing that was not yet desire, was so strong that she waited, almost in fear, for the moment when it would reach him and be recognised.

He humped the bedclothes and turned his back on her, mountainous. 'Well,' he said, 'good-night.'

After a minute she said, 'Good-night, Rex,' and turned on her side, away from him.

Chapter 38

ND HOW IS THAT DAUGHTER of yours, Mrs. Whiting? The one on the Vespa?'

She turned, almost knocking the drink out of his hand. Imperturbable, smiling like a lynx, Herb looked down on her.

It was Sunday, and Christmas had begun. They had come with their children. A herd of small girls neighed and pranced about the lawn, harnessed with string. Upstairs, boys in tweed suits and yellow waistcoats moodily played ping-pong or leafed through old copies of *Country Life*. A few older ones stayed with the party, getting in the way, eating crisps, their collars too tight or their tweed skirts too baggy. On the grand piano a white-and-silver Christmas tree trembled and shed its frost. Every surface was covered with Christmas cards. Guests looked for their own, and were offended when they found them obscured by other people's. Everyone on the Common was there, and they were drinking champagne. Their host was the literary agent, whom none of them really cared for.

'Oh. Hullo,' she said stupidly. And then, even more stupidly, 'Vespa?'

He undulated slightly, avoiding a small boy with a plate of canapes.

'I always remember you as someone waving after a Vespa.'

'Oh.' She stepped back into two young girls sitting side by side, speechless, on the sofa. They smiled briefly when she apologised. Herb stepped after her. He seemed unable to carry on a conversation at a distance of more than four inches.

'And how is,' she asked wildly, the name forgotten, 'your friend—the girl—the one you were with last time?'

'Oh, Maxine.' He nodded. His eyes were like mouths. 'Oh, she's not with me, dear. You don't have to worry.'

'Worry?'

'I'm here on my own.'

'But why should I worry?'

As he smiled, it suddenly occurred to her what he might mean. They were forced into a dreadful intimacy. He had followed her as she backed behind the sofa and they were now cut off from the rest of the party. What had Maxine told him? Was he the one who had paid Fickstein for Maxine? Why wouldn't Jane let me ask Maxine about a doctor? The idea of blackmail shot through her mind. Absurd. She returned to it cautiously, armed with disbelief.

'You haven't answered my question,' he murmured, eating her.

'What question? Oh, you mean Angela.'

'That's right.'

'She's fine. She's very well.'

'Is she here?'

'No. No, she's working.'

'She was working last time.'

'Was she? Well. She works very hard.'

'I think you keep her hidden. No competition. Is that it?'

'Don't be ridiculous.'

He cowered grotesquely. 'I'm sorry. It wasn't my fault, you know, dear. I did all I could. Don't take it out on me.'

'Are we talking about Angela? What are we talking about?'

'Oh, come, now. It's a nice morning, it's Christmas, there's plenty of champagne. Let it pass. How's your husband?'

'He's over there. Why don't you go and talk to him?' He would know from Jane that Rex hadn't been told. She leant against the back of the sofa. The little girls were rearing and whinnying, their front feet pawing the air.

'No, thanks.'

'Why not?'

'Skip it,' he said. He shrugged his thin shoulders and left her, weaving his way towards Jane. Julian, wearing his school suit, suddenly appeared behind Ruth's shoulder.

'They want us to stay for lunch,' he said gloomily.

'Do you want to?'

'Mike does. I don't.'

'Then don't.'

'I suppose if Mike is, I will.'

'Don't look so miserable. What's the matter?'

'Oh . . . nothing.'

She was left alone. She turned slowly and faced the room. This was the first time for months that she had met them all. They were different. Or was it that she was different? She no longer belonged to them. But had she ever belonged? Richard Tanner smiled faintly at her and turned his back. He would have waved, blown her a kiss, beckoned her over if he had not changed. It couldn't be because of Rackworth's party. It must be because they knew about Angela.

They all knew, and they were sorry for Rex because he was the only one who didn't know. His own daughter. The poor chap.

She began to cross the room cautiously, edging from group to group.

'Oh, hullo, Ruth. Well, she needed a decoke anyway—'

'Haven't seen you for ages, Ruth. I'm just going to get myself another glass of champers—'

'Feeling all right again? I do hope so. Well, when I got back she hadn't even begun the washing-up—'

'Well, Ruth. You're quite a stranger. How's the family?'

John Phillips, not avoiding her but standing four square in a scarlet waistcoat. She ducked her head, as though somehow she could get round him.

'They're well, thank you. I'm just—I'm just going.'

'You look all right.'

'Oh, I am.'

'And Angela?' He had lowered his voice; he wasn't looking at her.

'She's well too,' she said, slowly and clearly as though he were deaf.

'Everything—all right?'

'Perfectly all right.'

'You've been having a bad time,' he mumbled. 'I'm sorry.'

She was trembling. 'You could have helped. You didn't. You just gossiped, like the rest of them. I don't see what you're sorry for!'

'Good heavens, Ruth, what could *I* do? What could *I* do?'

'You could have kept your mouth shut!'

He stepped back, astounded. She pushed him away. Somebody very near her said, 'It's disgusting!', a violent denunciation. But nobody came after her. She pulled on her coat as she hurried across the gravel, through the gate, out on to the Common.

She walked quickly, leaving the car for Rex. The turf was brittle, thin, cellophane ice on the puddles, magpies and jays stiffly frozen on their gibbets. The din of church bells was remote, blanketed by the blue air. As she walked, with small steps and gloved hands, she seemed to be crying. There were no tears. She wanted to hit something, to slash the heads of the bracken. But she walked neatly, as though returning from church. She wanted to shout out loud, but tightened her lips . . . She began to run.

Chapter 39

AND AT LAST she began to run.

When Angela was six the family in the literary agent's house had employed a governess, a big, scrawny woman, vaguely unclean. So they had formed a little class, such a good idea, and the children had been deposited there at nine and fetched at twelve-thirty. They had been well-mannered, sickly children of eight or nine. Their parents had been the last generation of Commoners, now moved to flats in Palace Gate or retirement by the sea, the children married or, at any rate, grown.

Ruth had been twenty-four. Nursing a mewing, blotchy Julian, with half the floors up and creepers of raw flex sprouting from the middle of the ceilings. The Common, in those days, was a reunion: everyone trying to live as they had done before, to reorganise a club, to start things going. They pooled their sugar ration to make jam and kept nothing secret.

'I've arranged for Angela to go to this class. She can start on Monday.'

'But why?'

'Show support. All the other kids are going.'

'But they're much older!'

'She's six, isn't she? Take her on Monday.'

Bicycling, because they had no car, with Angela on the carrier. Leaving Julian with the people in the Tanners' house. Immense, now untraceable problems of time and washing and cooking and cleaning and bicycling, the dead weight behind her in tears, whether it was going or coming.

'Take her as far as the corner, then, and let her go by herself. It's a perfectly straight path. Good God, the child's not a baby.'

And one hot, scorched morning, with adders in the grass and the bracken terribly still, the people in the Tanners' house had gone to London. She had bicycled to the corner and, bending to Angela's level, pointed out the path. She had seen the forest of bracken, head-high. The child had moved off, hunched inside a small gingham dress, sandalled feet scuffing the sand.

Why had she followed her? Just as far as the twist in the path, when the bracken would hide her from view. Quietly, a few yards behind, in case she should fall, or go the wrong way. In case she should be frightened?

The child, thinking she was alone, had started to cry. At first it was little gasps and moans; then, mounting, a torrent of crying. She didn't stop, but plodded on as though driven. Ruth followed. She's all right, she told herself, she'll be all right. But she couldn't leave her. Neither could she call out. She walked behind, useless, witnessing an enormous agony. There, but not known to be there. And so, as far as Angela was concerned, not there at all.

After a little while the child had picked up a stick. To defend herself? No. To fight her way. Very small, desperate, she had slashed the bracken on either side.

'I'll never get there! I'll never get there!'

234

She thought nobody heard her. She beat the bracken, stumbling on all the time.

And where was she going to? The scrawny governess, who despised her; the neat children, who pinched her cunningly. Twenty yards from the house, the school, where the path ran straight to the front gate, Ruth had stopped. She could have run on and knelt and held the child, comforting her, promising a whole bounty of love. She could at least have said she was sorry. But she stopped, watching the child go on, watching her drop the stick and reach up for the latch of the gate. And for a moment, appallingly, she had felt a kind of pride.

'How did you get on this morning?'

'All right.'

'You didn't mind going alone?'

'No. I didn't mind.'

'Will you go alone tomorrow?'

'All right.

And at last, released by pity, anger and shame, she began to run. It had taken her twelve years. It had taken her all her life. At last she began to run.

Chapter 40

HE TRAIN WAS EMPTY. They were the only passengers. A steady rain fell on the coke and cinders, whipped against the iron struts, beat on the glass roof of the station. The platform was like a pier; the train moved slowly into a land and sky streaming with water.

'It's not a bit like Christmas.'

'No.'

'I'm glad, really.'

'Yes. I'm glad too.'

They did not look at each other, or smile.

'Phyllis Brigson worked wonders. He even gave me some money.'

'Don't be too hard on him.'

'I'm not.' She smiled shyly, glancing at her mother. 'He's just like Tony. They can't help it.'

'No. I know.'

'I used to think there was something *more* about Tony. You know, that he was going to give me a terrific surprise. But he never did. There just wasn't anything more. I mean —nothing.'

'You don't—you don't mind too much about him?'

'No. Not now.'

The train careered through the rain at enormous speed, pouring out steam and smoke. Signals fell, points changed, small stations streamed by, ravines of empty streets, paper streamers in one brilliantly lit room.

'Daddy didn't mind you coming?'

'No. I think he was rather glad. He likes being alone with the children.'

'Yes. I know. He likes being with them.'

'He feels—certain with them.'

'I know. Do you think that's why I'm different? I mean, because you weren't married?'

'No. You aren't any different. We were different to you, that's all.'

'Yes. Of course. You would be.' She looked down at her long, bare hands. 'I would be, too.'

'Don't let's talk about it any more.'

'Why?'

'Because now—I mean, now it's too difficult.'

'All right.'

'Did you remember your toothbrush?'

'Yes. But I took your toothpaste. The boys use that awful green stuff.'

Don't think whether you have done right. Nothing is right. The worst thing is to expect too much and not to know, not to be told, why you get so little. To be truthful with love is right.

'Don't worry.'

'I'm not worrying.'

'Yes, you are. You can't blame me for making a bit of a fuss when you told me.'

'Of course not.'

'You were quite right. Honestly you were.'

'I didn't think. I mean, I didn't think I was going to tell you.'

'I know. That's why you were right. You did it to help me. Well, it did, because you see—'

'Let's not talk about it now. Please.'

'All right.

Angela rubbed a clearing in the window.

'Do you know where it is? The nursing home?'

'Yes, I think so.

'Will Fickstein be there?'

'No. Not till this evening.'

'What will they do?'

'When?'

'I mean, how do they do it?'

'They—they just scrape out your womb. It's called a curettage. I think that's what they call it.'

'Does it hurt?'

'No. They'll give you an injection. You won't know anything about it.'

Angela became quiet. Oh, God, Ruth prayed, let it be over. No, not let it be over. Don't let her feel she's alone. Don't leave me alone. Don't let it happen at all.

Afterwards, Angela thought, I'll get my hair cut. I might have a perm. Just the ends.

'You know that dress you said you might buy me for Christmas?'

'What?'

'You said you might buy me a dress for Christmas.'

'Oh. Oh, yes.'

'Well, I wouldn't mind one. I mean, if you haven't got me anything already.'

'I have, actually.' The Works of Thomas Lovell Beddoes.

'Oh. It doesn't matter then.'

'But we'll get the dress too, if you like.'

'Thanks awfully.'

It isn't happening. It isn't Christmas Eve. We're going shopping for a dress. Harrods is so much easier. Expensive, I know, but I always think it's worth it. Put it down on my account: Mrs. Rex Whiting. Thank you, Mrs. Whiting. Now we'll have tea in the Silver Grill; no longer alone, but a mother and daughter like other mothers and daughters. I say, just look at that woman's hat. Angela says, let's go and buy you a new hat. We smile across the watercress sandwiches, the meringues like wedding cake . . .

'Will they shave me?' Angela asked.

'Will they—? Oh. Yes. I expect so.'

'I wish it was all over.

'Well, this time tomorrow it will be.'

'I know. This time tomorrow you'll all be in church.'

'In church?'

'He always makes us go at Christmas, doesn't he?'

'Yes. I suppose so. I'd forgotten.'

'You were married in church, weren't you?'

'Yes.'

'It's funny to think I was there. In a way, if you see what I mean. Did you wear white and all that?'

'No.'

'What did you wear?'

'A—sort of printed silk thing. A brown hat.'

'How depressing. Because of me, I suppose?'

'No, not because of *you*—my father—my parents were upset.'

'I bet they were. And you've never seen them since.'

'No. They've never been back from Ireland.'

'I often wondered about them. I mean, why we didn't go and stay. Other people's grandmothers—I suppose that's why Phyllis Brigson has one. Maybe she's really me.'

'Who?'

'Phyllis Brigson. I suppose it's about as far away as you can get—going to stay with your grandmother in Lichfield.'

'I'm sorry.'

'Oh, don't be sorry. I only minded when I didn't know. Honestly. You don't want to talk about it, though, do you?'

'Yes, of course, it's just that I've never talked about it, and just now, today . . . Have we passed Reading?'

'Ages ago. But you must have talked about it to him?'

'No.'

'But what did he feel about it? I mean, what did he feel about me?'

'I don't know. What would Tony feel?'

'He doesn't feel anything, except when he wants to go to bed, or he's angry, or when he thinks people don't like him.'

'Then that's the answer.'

'But you had Julian, then you had Mike. I mean, why?'

'Julian was after the war. Mike was—I don't know, to show that we could afford it, everyone else on the Common was having babies. He thought Mike would be a girl.'

'That's no reason. You wanted them. Didn't you?'

'Yes, of course.'

'You always seemed to love them so much.'

'I do. Of course I do.'

'Then didn't they make up for—me and everything?'

'I wish you'd stop saying *you*. It wasn't *you*.'

'But it was once I was born.'

'He was—it's hard to explain—jealous of them. He lived at home then. Well, you remember.'

'No.'

'I suppose you were at school . . . Look, the rain's stopping. Where are we?'

'How do you mean, jealous of them?'

'He thought I was making them, I don't know, soft. You don't kiss boys, you don't pick them up, boys don't cry. Well, there were always scenes. Every night. At the weekends. It was years ago. Really, I don't remember.'

'Yes, you do. So he sent them off to boarding school, so he could have you to himself.'

'No, not to himself. I mean, he's very fond of them, you mustn't think . . . He just didn't want me to be. When they'd gone, it was easier for him. He didn't think I was—'

'Plotting behind his back. Having a nicer time with them than you were with him. God, what a fool he is.'

'No, he isn't. You mustn't dislike him—'

'I don't dislike him. I just think he's a fool. I don't care about him at all any more.'

'But—'

'I don't. I don't have to live with him. Or with Tony, thank God. I feel—gosh, I feel absolutely wonderful.'

'I'm glad.'

'Oh, I suppose that sounds awful. But I do. Poor old Mum, you must have had a ghastly time. I suppose you should have aborted me, really. Not that I'm glad you didn't. Although I suppose if you never know, it's all right. Rather depressing to think of, really.'

'Yes. It is.'

'Now I've upset you. I'm sorry.'

'You haven't. I wish it was all different.'

'Well, after this is over it will be. It'll be quite different. Honestly.'

'Yes . . . Yes, I'm sure it will.'

'That's better.'

'We might go somewhere at Easter,' Ruth said after a moment. 'Abroad somewhere. I'm sure Miss de Beer would come and look after the boys.'

'Oh, she's crazy for them. They like her too, I must say I can't think why.'

'Shall we do that, then?'

'Well . . . well, we might. I don't know.'

'We're nearly there.'

'We are there. Come on.'

She stepped out of the train with her canvas grip; turned to help Ruth down. Am I an old woman? A Christmas tree towered above the shuffling, macintoshed crowds. 'I'm dreaming,' bellowed the loudspeakers, 'of a white Christmas—' The taxi-driver had hung a sprig of mistletoe over the back seat.

'I suppose Fickstein doesn't have Christmas.'

'No.'

'It must seem awfully silly, to people who don't have it.'

'No sillier than Passover or something does to us.'

'Well, I mean, that's different.'

What are we talking about? Why aren't we thinking about what is going to happen? We're taking a child to be killed. It lies so still, hidden. Don't think like that, because it doesn't mean anything any more. This child lived. And says she is feeling wonderful. Could I take her hand? She must know that I'm glad.

'Anyway,' she began painfully, 'I'm glad—'

Angela swivelled round, peered out of the back window.

'That's the sort of dress I'd like, in that shop. You know, quite plain with a low neck and three-quarter-length sleeves. It was sort of mauve.'

'Mauve?'

'I say, look at that.' Noddies and gnomes gyrating with maniac precision in a forest of potted firs. Santa Claus large as God bowing and smiling and giving nothing away. Angels with silent trumpets. Clowns shaking with silent laughter. A church with its huge, prophetic cross twinkling red, green and purple.

'Did you get a tree?' Angela asked.

'Yes, he's—Daddy's getting it today.'

'I suppose you'll decorate it this evening.'

'I expect so.'

'Oh, well. I don't mind, really. I hope the kids have a nice time.'

'I'm sure they will.'

The taxi stopped in front of a large private house. Rain pitted the gravel, soaked the well-clipped evergreens.

'Are we here?'

'I suppose so.'

Unbelieving, they climbed out, stood in the rain while Ruth paid the driver. It was several minutes before anyone answered the bell.

'Good morning?'

'Good morning. I've brought my—Miss Whiting.'

'Oh. Yes. Doctor Fickstein's patient. Will you come in?'

The hall was Tudor, hung with paper bells and balls and stars. A neat, glowing fire burned in the ornate grate. There was a visitor's book and an artificial Christmas tree. The nurse went away. There was complete silence.

'I think it's empty,' Angela whispered. 'Or else they're all dead.'

'It seems quite nice.'

'I thought there'd be bedpans and things. You know. Dettol.'

It was impossible to whisper in the silence. They sat back on their tapestried chairs. Suddenly Angela leant forward.

'What about the money?'

'It's all right. I've got it.'

'But how? Where from?'

'I was going to Antibes,' Ruth said. 'He gave me two hundred pounds.'

'But doesn't he want that back?'

'It was a present.'

'But won't he ask about it?'

'Of course.' Ruth smiled quickly. Both of them seemed to hear the remote sound of Rex's shouting: thin, meaningless as the howls of somebody else's child. 'But you know,' she said, 'I'm hopeless about money. Hopeless.'

Angela said, 'Oh . . .' leaning towards her with pity, a sudden feeling of shame. A grey woman with uncertain eyes came running down the stairs, holding out her hand as though to welcome them to a prize-giving. Angela stood up.

'Miss Whiting?' the woman asked. 'Mrs. Whiting? What a nasty day.'

She knows what we're here for, Ruth warned, swiftly, unreasonably protective. Don't trust her. Don't stay with her. Let's go away.

But Angela, with deference and good manners, was shaking her hand. She seemed completely at ease.

'I am Miss Holliwell. Now if you will bring your bag, dear—'

'Yes, Miss Holliwell.' She began to follow the woman up the stairs. Ruth hurried after them.

They climbed. They were going to the attics. Angela, Ruth called soundlessly. Come back.

'Sometimes,' Miss Holliwell panted, 'when I have to run up these stairs to the labour ward I think I'll never get there. Unfortunately it's impossible to have a lift owing to the construction of—' She gave up. They plodded on in single file. The rain beat down on a skylight.

'Now this is your room, dear. Nice and near the theatre. I think you'll be comfortable.'

A dark cupboard, its cracked window looking out on a brick wall. An iron bedstead. Peeling paint. Brown stains in the basin. *No,* Ruth cried.

'It's fine,' Angela said. 'Thank you.'

'I should get into bed now. Nurse will bring you some lunch at twelve-thirty.'

'Up all those stairs?' Ruth asked wildly.

Both Angela and Miss Holliwell looked at her.

'Of course,' Miss Holliwell said.

'Is there a bell? Has she got a bell?'

'It was out of order. The electricians are attending to it.'

'But what happens if she wants something?'

'There is always a nurse on duty.'

'Up here? All the time?'

'Oh, really, Mummy,' Angela said, 'I'll be all right.'

'Is there a telephone?'

Angela sighed dismally.

'No,' Miss Holliwell said, 'I'm afraid not. This room is not normally in use, but since we are quite full up and Doctor Fickstein said it was urgent—'

'Yes,' Ruth said. 'I see.' She sat down on the edge of the bed. The springs whined.

'Doctor Fickstein will be here about nine o'clock,' Miss Holliwell spoke directly to Angela. 'So you can take things easy today, can't you? Plenty to read, I hope?'

'So late?' Ruth asked, with little hope.

'The operating theatre is in use all day, Mrs. Whiting. We have three mothers going neck-and-neck. We must wait until they are tidied away. It's a case of priority.'

You mean the labour ward becomes the operating theatre. Everything thrown together into the same . . . She looked desperately up at Angela. She was unzipping her bag.

'Well,' Miss Holliwell said, 'I must get back to my babies. I'll see you this evening, dear.'

'Yes, Miss Holliwell.'

In the silence, Angela unpacked her sponge bag and slippers. I'm not helping her, Ruth thought. I've done this so often before. You get up and you say briskly, 'Well, darling, we'll be seeing you again before we know where we are.' You say, 'Well, I'd better be going now.' And you look as though you had somewhere to go. You don't cry or cling or say, 'Come back. Don't stay here.' You get up—like this —and smile—like this—and clear the ache in your throat with a silly, nervous cough.

'Well, darling . . . I'd better be getting along.'

'Yes.'

'I'll telephone tonight to see how you are.'

'Oh, I shouldn't bother.'

'And we'll expect you on Friday.'

'Yes.'

'You've got everything you want?'

'Yes, thank you.

'Well—'

'You don't understand,' Angela said gently. 'I *want* this done. I'm happy. Just think, tomorrow I'll wake up and it'll all be over. I can't wait. I'm *happy*. You see?'

'Yes,' Ruth said. 'Well, good-bye, then.'

She reached up. The child dwarfed her. Then she was hurrying down the stairs, hurrying along the wet road, turning corners, turning into other roads, the rain slapping her face, the roads leading somewhere, they must lead somewhere.

What have I done? What have I done? Not, what am I going to do, but oh God, what have I done?

Chapter 41

WELL,' THE ticket collector said, 'we could have done with this at Christmas.'

Beyond the station entrance snow whirled in a soft, harmless blizzard.

'Yes,' Ruth said, holding out her glove. 'Yes, we could.'

'The young gentlemen get off all right?'

'Oh, yes, thank you.'

'Must be five years now I've been watching them go off. Grow up fast, don't they?'

'Yes, they do.'

'Seems funny without them at first, I suppose?'

'Yes, it does.'

She balanced her parcels and started off towards the station entrance. For a moment she hesitated in front of the snow, standing on the brink of it.

'You're not driving in this, Mrs. Whiting?'

She looked up. A parcel slipped and she caught it awkwardly. Rackworth looked like a gaunt trapper. He seemed, as though finding her tottering across the Arctic, genuinely concerned.

'Oh, yes. It's not so bad, really.'

'I'm just seeing some friends off. I'll give you a lift, if you don't mind waiting a few minutes.'

'No, thank you. I'll be all right, really.'

'Angela's gone back to Oxford, I suppose?'

'Yes, she went yesterday.'

'She's a very bright girl.' He smiled gently between the fur collar and the peaked hat. 'We've enjoyed seeing her over the last couple of weeks.'

'I hope,' faintly, wildly, clutching at a falling parcel, 'I hope she wasn't a nuisance.'

'You mean you hope she didn't break things and pee on the carpet?' He laughed sadly, looking at her as though she were a mistake. 'No, she wasn't. She's a very bright girl. We liked seeing her.'

There was nothing more to be said. The commuters straggled past, hats down, collars up, shoulders hunched in the last stages of a retreat.

'Well,' Ruth said, 'I must—'

'She tells me she's getting a job next vacation. If she doesn't, she's welcome to come down any time.'

'Thank you, but I expect,' she had never heard of it before, 'I expect she'll get a job. Good-bye, Mr. Rackworth.'

The car was iced, shapeless in the empty car park. She scraped the snow off the windows with both hands. When she got into the car she blew on her hands, wrung them, tried to dry them on her coat. As she turned the car, cautiously with its load of snow, the Jaguar purred quietly away, became a small red beacon and disappeared.

At first the problems of the dark and the snow took all her attention. She sat stiffly peering through a semicircle of glass into an unrecognisable future; she turned the tightly clasped wheel this way and that to follow a road she remembered. Later, when she turned on the headlights and began to climb up the narrow road through the woods, she slipped down a little in her seat, blew on her hands again. The hot, damp air from the heater melted her skin. The windscreen wipers hummed, hypnotic as metronomes.

You will drive home. It will be winter. You will be older.

It's over, she told herself. They have all gone. You are driving home, it's winter and you are older.

How long had she believed it would be different? A week? Looping the tinsel, folding the wrapping-paper, singing in church, Mike's clear soprano and the holy glint in his eye: the child was dead, but Angela was alive. She had gone back to the beginning, and Angela was hers. At last I love her, and she trusts me, and I'm justified. She held up her head and sang with her small, flat voice. When Rex looked at her she smiled, making him look again to discover who she was under the church-going hat.

A week? Hardly that. There had been Christmas presents for Angela when she came home; a tree of her own, because she had missed it. The children, even Rex, were infected with happiness, the need for a tremendous welcome. They received her back from Phyllis Brigson and Lichfield as though she had won some extraordinary prize. She looked as though she had won a prize: pale, tired, but radiant. Angela was sometimes cheerful. She had never been radiant. Rex supposed it was the air. He kept looking at her, and when she noticed him she smiled. He supposed, on second thoughts, that she was in love.

She's relieved, Ruth told herself. Of course she is. There's nothing else. She waited for Angela to talk to her; she waited to make plans. She waited, but the days raced by, they were hardly ever alone. If they were, they discussed Angela's new clothes, Angela's hair—and then, light, quick, almost graceful, she was gone. She spent whole days with Julian and Mike away from the house.

'Where have you been?'

'On the tractor.'

'What tractor?'

'Up at Bankside. It's one of Ralph's farms.'

'And what did Angela do?'

'Oh, she went back to Ralph's for lunch.'

'Didn't you go?'

'No, they gave us some of their sandwiches. I say, do you know he let her drive the Jag?'

'Who? *Angela?*'

She didn't exactly avoid Ruth, but she was always on her way somewhere; touching her, smiling as she passed, but always going. She doesn't exactly avoid me, Ruth thought. It's as though she didn't notice me any more. She goes through me, not round me. As though—which of course isn't true—I no longer existed for her.

But I have only just begun to exist.

As though—which of course is absurd—she had grown up.

But she has only just begun to be a child.

Then Angela went away. Nothing had happened. There had been no incident, no sudden revelation. It was time for her to go back, and she went, fetched by a young man in a Morris Minor with 'Betsy II' painted on the bonnet; a plain, silent young man in rimless glasses called Jack.

But for the first time she had luggage. Her bedroom was stripped of everything, pictures, ornaments, cushions, even the waste-paper basket was gone. She had taken all her clothes and left only the medical student's sweater, the skirt with the safety-pin inextricably hooked into the frayed tweed.

She had, in fact, moved. She had gone as quietly and purposefully as leaving a hotel in which she had spent a long night of childhood.

It was not until she had gone that Ruth realised it clearly. Her hand was still raised, although they were not waving; her lips still forming 'Good-bye,' although they were looking ahead and had already forgotten. This time she will never come back.

There was nowhere to put a belated love, a small, painfully achieved humanity. A fussy little woman with too many parcels, she drove correctly and carefully home to an empty world, slowing up at corners, meticulously indicating left and right to the following and approaching darkness. What remained?

Rex. Rex remained. Even Miss de Beer had gone, leaving four hairpins on the dressing-table and a religious calendar. But Rex was still there.

He had a bad cold. He thought he was going to die.

The world was empty. But tiny, minutely raging, the figure of Rex was pin-pointed, the sole survivor. Rex sneezing, with terrible, diminutive force. Rex gargling to protect his throat. Rex blowing his nose. Rex taking his temperature and feeling his pulse. Rex suffering.

She tried to feel glad that Rex would be there. She tried to worry about whether he was worse, or better, warm enough, sufficiently supplied with handkerchiefs. In the next few minutes she had to travel an immense distance, from herself to Rex: from her own desolation to Rex's cold.

She must prepare for it somehow, defend herself somehow. She couldn't face him like this, sober, with no cunning with nothing in her mind but truth.

Isn't there a game I can play? Pretend that I'm . . .

No, there is nothing.

Shall I go to the Tanners'? Talk about Robert's divorce and Baby's back teeth and the rumour that Meg Wilmington-Smith is pregnant at last. . . .

No. It's all over. You can't go back. You can only go on to the end, which is this gate, this white lawn with yesterday's snowmen standing in the dark.

Yes. I suppose so. I suppose so. And yet . . .

She stopped the car in the garage, switched off the engine. The headlamps glared on bicycles thrown against the wall. The snow fell, thudding softly from the roof of the garage.

And yet why? Why must I come back?

You're getting confused again.

I'm free. I don't have to get out of this car. I don't have to come back.

You're getting confused with Angela again. It's Angela who's free. She doesn't owe anything.

Neither do I.

Then prove it. All you have to do is turn the key.

But where shall I go?

To another dream, another hiding-place.

But the dreams have all gone. The hiding-places aren't there.

So you must live without them.

And pay? Pay for everything?

At last. From your heart, for everything.

She slumped over the steering wheel, her head on her arms. She had no nobility and little courage. Inadequate, commonplace, no longer young, she found the burden of consequence too heavy. It crushed her.

Please let me rest. Let me stay here forever. Let me rest.

It was the last evasion, an unanswered, unanswerable prayer. The snow slipped and fell. The snowmen lurched, slid quietly to the ground.

Finally she sat up. She smoothed her hair. She gathered up her parcels one by one, her hat and gloves, her trivial armour. Avoiding the carelessly abandoned bicycles, the gum boots, she went into the house.

.

caveofice00mort

caveofice00mort

caveofice00mort

Printed in the USA
CPSIA information can be obtained
at www.ICGtesting.com
LVHW021258221023
761792LV00003B/156